TIM SEPPANEN'S

FIRES FAR DISTANT

a novel

EXSEPT

This edition ©2022
Timothy Ronald Seppanen
All rights reserved.

Cover photo: Tim Seppanen

Dedicated to my father,
Ronald Paul Seppanen.
30 years. Miss you Dad.

And to my daughter,
Aurora Jane, my light and bright,
shining hope for the future

Prologue

Shots rang out at me as I raced down the narrow hallways of the old motel, half-crouching in the gray chaos that spilled from the devouring flames above and around me. Screams echoed from an ill-formed distance, and I heard the shouts of deeper voices pounding in the confines of that particular small corner of hell.

A voice sounded in my headset, calm amidst the chaos: "Number Three, we have 10 women, more are still in there. Three, use caution, it looks like the roof is ready to go. You should get out of there."

I pounded on, trying to hold my breath, slamming into doors, only to carom across the hall into another. A kick from a plated boot, a yell, a scan of another smoky room, then another.

Intelligence had filtered to our team that the group we had been tracking for the past year had been holding court in an old, abandoned motel that was more a compartmentalized warehouse than accommodation. A group of women, mostly illegal aliens, were being held against their will, packaging and cutting drugs along with a litany of other forced horrors.

I heard voices faint and seemingly far away in the swirling

smoke and chaos. Hands reached out, grasping. Coughing and weight, staggering, and finally . . . oblivion.

Chapter 1

The blows rained heavily upon the broken body as a short but powerfully-muscled man pounded with fury on the near lifeless figure. The sounds of the fists striking flesh were interspersed by that of ragged gasps, then moans, then nothing as the slumped figure sank to the ground. The strong hands of two men who had held him erect to absorb the punishment finally let the bruised and battered husk down into ash.

Thunder rolled overhead, and deep echoes found their way into the small hollow of the homestead. Lightning crashed, illuminating the devastation. Men worked with horses, pulling down a corral; animals screamed as they were shot.

Two young girls were dragged by faceless men into the clearing in front of the cabin. Jagged streaks of light lit up one family's nightmare. The tearful pleas of the young women were silenced by gauntleted hands.

The powerful man looked up from the handkerchief he was using to wipe blood from his hands, and his words were a soulless knife's edge against the terror of that black night.

"That will be the last you will see of your father. He was foolish to stand against us." He mounted his horse, motioned to the others, and shouted over his shoulder: "Burn it all."

***

The line of horsemen moved through the night, with occasional curses from men as low-hanging branches whipped their faces. Rain streaked from the skies, a torrent of condemnation on the black figures. There was a whisper of sound, and one man fell from his horse with a heavy thud, splattering mud and leaves. The man behind him dismounted with an oath and yelled through the wind and rain to his comrades as he reached down to turn over the body. With difficulty, he lit a match close against his chest; the illuminated face was streaked with blood, which poured from the base of a knife haft buried in his neck. He dropped the match, startled, and looked up to see his last as a violent darkness closed about him.

Ahead on the trail, low murmurs rose from the closed rank of men. One whispered to a rider behind him: "I don't like taking women, it doesn't feel right. I didn't sign up for this."

A harsh hiss of words fell upon him. "Dusty, what did you think we were doing there at that homestead? Why don't you shut your mouth and keep your thoughts to yourself." The words were the last he would speak. He fell to the ground, lifeless, his horse rearing from the impact and force of the falling men.

Dusty whirled in his saddle, gun in hand.

"What the . . .?" He heard nothing but the force of water that poured from the skies, striking trees, branches, and the earth around the trail. The petrichor of the night overtook him as well; his last sight in life was a flash of red and blazing eyes that moved across his field of vision.

The girls had given up struggling, each slumped now in the arms of their captors, one barely breathing. A fleshy man with a limp mustache held his reins and a strong hand upon the brunette. A taller blond man with a weak chin had an arm around a listless and small-framed blond. The two were sisters, and their heads sunk forward, as if in a daze or dream. They would wake to a nightmare.

***

Ezekiel O'Reilly awoke deep underwater, fought his way to the mental surface, and gasped in the shrouded mist of the dark morning. He struggled to get to his feet, only to find his body and legs would not let him. He crawled to the smoking ashes of the cabin, ignoring the sirens of unconsciousness that begged him to fall back into oblivion. He frantically tore at charred timbers, sifting through the wreckage of what once was his home, choking on the taste of cold sulfur.

He could feel the life coursing from him. He clutched his chest, on his knees in the middle of the scarred remains of his life. He clawed through smoking timbers, searching for his gun. He needed to go after the horsemen, to rescue his daughters. His hands were horribly burnt, torn from ragged nails and the coals that still lingered in the smoking ruins.

He cast his eyes heavenward and screamed a prayer. He lifted his arms, noticing that they felt very heavy.

9

Gentle hands and strong arms caught him as he started to topple. The hands gently carried him over to some taller grass, and a bundle of cloth was placed under his head. He felt cold water trickle into his charred lips, and he drank greedily, coughing as it mixed with the ash he had inhaled. He tried to lift a hand to clear his eyes and found he could not. It seemed as if his eyes were clouded.

"Who —" The word was uttered feebly, and he clutched at the supporting arms.

"Zeke, it's me." The words were resonant and seemed to hit hollow chords in his consciousness.

"Eli?"

"Zeke, I'm sorry. I caught up with them, but two men and their boss escaped. I got four of them."

"The girls?" Zeke's own voice felt distant, and he swore he heard music somewhere far distant.

"I will find them, Zeke, I promise. I'm sorry I wasn't here. I left Kansas as soon as I got your letter."

"Please, avenge me. Save Cassie and Theresa. Please, Eli." He was fading, with his words trailing off.

"I will," his brother reassured. "Even to the ends of the earth. I will avenge you."

A crash of thunder was followed by a desperate stillness as the ragged breathing subdued to a harsh whisper, which then grew ever quieter, until it was no more.

Chapter 2

The night was still warm, but whispers of the coming winter were in the air. Crickets sang in the trees surrounding the railroad depot, and the leaves of aspens clapped enthusiastically in the currents of wind. The atmosphere was brooding and self-aware, tinged with the smoke of distant fires. The last fringes of a golden twilight edged the western horizon and waited for night to completely close its curtain on the last of its singing chords. The veil of darkness settled uneasily on the small town here in October 1907.

Joseph Alston remained standing on the baggage platform, taking in the last glimmer of daylight and sighing with creation and the hiss of the boilers in the lumber mills just south of the depot. He was a man of medium height, with a trimmed mustache, neatly kept, carrying the air of a man always keenly aware of his surroundings and his place within them. He was an entrepreneur, businessman, former postmaster, land agent, and local official. Very little happened in this small town he and his brother David had platted along the Mineral Range Railroad that he did not know about. This small community had formerly been known as Laird, although the local township and main roads of the community still bore the name.

He was an outwardly contented man, but his uneasy shifting of weight and position even while standing still belied an inward restlessness, a man always on the lookout for something else and the next business opportunity.

A match flared in the darkness, and the halo of light illuminated a sharp, angular face shadowed by cupped hands and a hat-brim pulled down.

Joseph was curious about the man. He was even more on guard against the aura of menace and danger he seemed to represent as a stranger in a small mill town in the middle of the Upper Michigan forest. He still heard nothing from the strange figure, not even the sounds of breathing.

"Nice evening." His own words sounded foreign in the silence, and he was only partially aware that he himself had actually spoken them to the dark figure. Nothing.

"Where are you from?" Again, the only response was the whisper of Mill Creek lapping and moving along its banks.

Joseph inhaled and used a thumb and forefinger to smooth his mustache and reached around his neck to remove his shopkeeper's apron. Eva, his wife, would be waiting with supper for him back behind the store. He turned away

"I am looking for a girl." The words were spoken plainly, carrying no melody or inflection, doing nothing to dispel the unformed miasma of danger descending on the platform.

Joseph turned. "A girl? Who?"

"I have been given to understand that there are girls who entertain in this area." The words were almost a hiss, low and cutting.

Joseph felt the heat rise to his cheeks. "I don't know what kind of town you think Alston is, I think you should look elsewhere. We are a lumber town; we only have churches, saloons, boarding houses, and stores. I think you should head west."

"I don't know what kind of town this is," the man retorted. "But where there are logging and railroad crews, one can often find a girl to talk to."

The edge and tone were enough to send a slight chill down Joseph's back. "I am sorry, you might ask around the mill tomorrow." There was no reply. The man was gone. All that remained was the lingering half-imagined image of a tall, lean, and dangerous shadow. He sure had a story to share with Eva over supper.

He moved to leave the platform but was halted by a more familiar form. The man before him appeared to have been hewn from rock — one could even imagine the chisel marks outlining his frame. His features were angular but proportioned on a massive scale. The corded neck muscles taxed the collar of the shirt he wore. He was easily close to seven feet tall, in an era when the average height of a man was well below six. The closely cropped hair looked like it had been chiseled from stone as well and was dark with highlights of grey.

"Who were you talking to, Joe?" the giant rumbled.

"Don't know who it was, he was just asking for directions, Danny."

"Maybe you should just ignore people like that, Joe. People

have a way of getting hurt by information."

Joseph sighed and stepped off the platform, no longer enjoying a beautiful evening.

"Have a good night, Joe. Say hi to Eva," the deep voice called after him.

Chapter 3

Sara Corbett stared out through the corner of the window visible from her bed. She clutched a thin quilt to her chest and cried silently. She was always shivering. The thin plank walls bled cold and dust. The lean-to room in which she was held captive was barely six feet by ten feet. If she made any sound, he would come in and beat her. She stretched out as far as the manacle chained to the wall would allow and strained to see more of the tiny rectangle of grey sky through her window. Her efforts were undertaken solely for a better view of the uplifted branches of the huge White Pine in the yard. Its huge boughs hung out at an impossible distance, seeming to defy gravity. She looked to them as a symbol of strength. She named it the Praying Tree because she kept it in her mind's eye as a symbol of supplication. The uppermost branches looked for all the world like arms raised to the heavens. It was a small representation of hope in the pit of deepest despair. She would gaze out the window, bracing herself against the sound of the shift whistle at the lumber mill. The whistle meant that men were done working, and soon some of them would come to the shack. She kept the image in her heart of upraised branches imploring the sky for deliverance.

She screamed inwardly at the echoing whistle, and silently began the countdown of minutes. She would hear rough voices, the tread of heavy feet on rough plank floors, and stare in horror as the door would open to her cell and darkness would overtake her again.

She awoke with the clattering of the latch as he came in — a daily featureless evil. He never spoke, just brought meager food, a bit of oatmeal and bread, a bucket for her needs, and as always, the threat of a heavy fist. He was lean and sallow-faced with bottomless black pools for eyes. His breath always stank, she assumed from his half-rotted teeth. He always wore black broadcloth trousers with suspenders and a dirty white collared shirt buttoned up to a stubbled weak chin.

She dreamed as always of home. Her mother would be baking bread, the smell filling the house with a delicious aroma. Her sisters would be laughing, making their sleepy way downstairs. Lisa would always grab her foot and tease, "Sleepyhead, wake up." She remembered sights, sounds, and the warmth of the fire. There would be lingering scents in the house, a tang of cinnamon, a hint of brown sugar . . . She remembered her mother hugging her good morning. She remembered peace and security, but all were ashes in her mouth now.

The forced ride on horseback and days of endless rain had only heightened her torment. Her iron-grey cell had held her for months. She was never allowed to go outside. In the near distance, she could hear the frenzied cries of packs of coyotes descending on another kill. She would weep, knowing how the deer would suffer. But the deer would know only an instant of pain, and then be no more. Her suffering knew no end, and she would know again and again the hands of her predators.

Sara knew there was a girl kept in an adjacent room which she assumed was similar to hers; she had heard the young woman's pleas and cries through the thin plank walls. Her crying was piteous, and Sara wished she could reach out and comfort her as well. But talking was forbidden, and Sara had endured the heavy hand of punishment many times when she tried to whisper out to the girl. They had tried to devise a system of taps to try and communicate somehow, but beyond a few taps of understanding, they had been unable to progress without meeting to come up with a cogent framework of "speaking."

So Sara would cry a bit louder, offer a few taps and hope to have the girl respond in kind. She would pretend she was a big sister, and pray that somehow she could absorb some of the girl's pain through the walls and carry silent comfort in the damp night air, a whisper of hope somewhere in the wilderness of pain. She would try, but knew they would both struggle on in their personal darkness, waiting for help and salvation. Night once again overtook her small square of window, and she steeled herself against the wave of pain she knew would soon come.

Chapter 4

The mill was a hive of activity, the groaning of the steam boiler was heard in between the nail-biting shrieks of the buzzsaw. Men would yell, and clouds of sawdust swirled and danced in the hazy sunlight.

A lean stranger could be seen walking to the mill manager's house across the sunbaked yard.

Hank Glassett, the mill foreman, looked up from his desk as the stranger entered, taking in the lean frame, the dark and deep-set eyes. It almost looked like he was perpetually in a shadow and that the cast of his countenance was impenetrable by light.

Hank was a florid man, sandy-red hair cut close on a round head, well under six feet tall, with powerful shoulders and a stomach that belied years of being a boss, much of which was spent behind a desk. He made a vague gesture towards a chair in front of the desk, an aged and worn contrivance that may have once passed as a secure place to sit.

"Are you doing any hiring?" The visitor's voice was flat, a whip-like crack across the dust-laden air.

"Only for general labor," Hank responded. The millwright, sawyer, and teamster positions are all filled." He reached for a smoldering cigar, scowled at the ash tray, thought better of it, and snuffed it out "Pay is $1.50 a day, 10-hour shifts, start at 7:00. No smoking on the premises, paychecks here every other Friday. You don't work hard, you're gone."

He barely looked up, suddenly caught up in a random entry in the open ledger in front of him. A fly circled lazily, avoiding a half-hearted swing of his heavy hand. "If you want to work, sign or put your mark on this agreement, then go see Danny in the yard."

The stranger leaned forward and made an "X" on a short line underscored at the bottom of the yellowed sheet, holding down a curled corner as he made the two slashes. They were much like the man who signed: sharp, angular, direct, and to the point.

"What is your name, stranger?"

The voice arced from the yard as the screen door squealed shut. "Zeke"

Danny watched as the man walked out of the yard, his face twisted into an approximation of a half-smile, as much the tectonic movements of his granite face could so be called. He rubbed his chin with the back of his hand. He would bide his time, but he had an appointment to keep. His searching stare was a mixture of cunning and wariness.

Chapter 5

The day dawned breathlessly, with a reverential hush that accompanied the light's movements across the fields and forests. My dogs pulled anxiously on their leashes, eager to follow the scent of a lingering night on the path ahead of us. I paused to take in the flood of light and its long shadows that lifted skyward, pondering the pure poetry of the moment how my life had changed so dramatically in recent years. I caught myself, as the man who had moved back here would not have been so easily taken by poetry, let alone ponder his world in such terms. My morning walks before moving back home — when there was time to take one — were often taken on concrete and asphalt. The morning mists were most often exhaust fumes from gridlocked cars, and my travels often took me into areas that often included some dangerous people. The years living downstate had honed some necessary and unusual skills, but it was good to let the landscape, smell, and feel of home wash over me. I had seen the world, and it often had stared back at me with bleak eyes. There were nights I relived moments of violence, and awoke in a cold sweat as old scars, both mental and physical, made their presence known. The scars of old burns ached, but they were matched too by the scars of memory: gunfire, flames, chaos . . . and the screams.

After a year of surgeries, and years of rehab, it still took time to adjust to disability and semi-retirement.

It had been nearly two years since I had moved back to my hometown with my wife, and I was reminded on mornings such as these why I had never regretted my move back following the death of my Uncle Jack. The small town of Alston in western Upper Michigan had long been a place to leave. Now, it was a place to call home. The air was clean and fresh, and I especially enjoyed the early morning walks in the 80 acres left to my family and me.

Uncle Jack was always telling me it was time to come home. I made yearly pilgrimages back to the U.P., and would sit on the porch of the old family farmhouse with Jack. We would drink his "lemonade" out of mason jars, although I believe the homemade beverage had all but lemonade in it. It was the stories I remembered most. He was a born storyteller, blending more often than not a mixture of fact, fiction, half-whispered truths, and a fair share of rumor and innuendo.

He told me my parents had named me Constantine after the Roman emperor who ruled from 306 A.D. to 337 A.D. and had been the first emperor to convert to Christianity. He converted on his deathbed but played an important role in the spread of Christianity by proclaiming religious tolerance for the faith throughout His Empire. He called the first council of Nicea, from which the Nicene Creed came. Jack said my middle name, John, was of course after my father — a dark and taciturn man, very much the antithesis of his brother, Jack. Our shared last name, Smith, was an Anglicized version of the family name my great-grandfather had brought from Finland. My mother Jane, Jack related, had been a quiet woman from near Lansing, and had met my father while on vacation with her family at their camp on South Laird Road. I had only vague memories of them, which I always thought was something I would need to deal with at some point in my life. I do remember being loved, and remember being held and hugged often.

We would often sit in the fading half-light of a northern summer, and I would listen. He told stories of scandal of years past: pregnant teenage girls who had "gone away" for a summer, returning with a baby, as well as suicides, mysterious deaths, ghosts and "h'ants" around the small community. He had been good friends with quite a few "old-timers," Finnish immigrants and farmers who would always share another story of the railroad and lumbering days for a bottomless cup of strong coffee and a piece of Nisu, a Finnish cardamom bread. There were hints of robbery, even a stagecoach robbery at the turn of the last century, before the railroad "came to town."

I would sit, rapt with attention at the local Native American legend of the Great Spirit that guarded a treasure in nearby Silver Mountain. Silver Mountain, six miles due south from the sleepy town of Alston, was a low "mountain" that rose above the Sturgeon River Gorge, a natural monument among a sandy plain of pine and maple. Silver had been prospected in nearby creeks, and a small mine had been bored into the mountain, but it was long blocked-off. No silver of any quantity had ever been found, although rumors circulated a century past that small molds for silver had been found, along with a few charms and crucifixes. Mysteriously, a nearby river was called Silver River, and there was even a small community called Silver sprung up on what came to be called South Laird Road. It seemed odd to me that with barely any silver being found, considering so many places and landmarks were given the name. The Spirit that guarded Silver Mountain supposedly cursed many who tried to search out the treasure.

There was a recounting of stories of "shady ladies," gambling, and even murder. I had often scoffed that the sleepy town of a few hundred people had ever known vice at that level, or known true evil at all. After years on the force, I came to know the depth of human depravity, a dark knowledge that would threaten my very sanity and rip my life asunder.

Therein lies my story: some poetry, some anguish, some secrets, and some dark observations that passed for my sense of humor.

Chapter 6

I first brought my now-wife Lauren home to meet Jack ten years ago. My smiling girlfriend, a brunette study in lithe elegance, was a sharp contrast to the outwardly hard-bitten farmer that had raised me. I watched them converse with interest.

His wife had died when I was very young. Marie had passed in childbirth, as did their stillborn daughter. He rarely spoke of them, but I would catch his wistful sadness when he passed the patch of wild roses he planted near the front porch steps following the death of his childhood sweetheart. I would sometimes catch him wiping away a tear as he would turn, embarrassed that I noticed his ritual of stopping near the roses and inhaling deeply, often dropping to a knee as if in prayer. I often wonder if his heart had finally failed after decades of sadness and lost love, even knowing that same heart, along with his work ethic, personal pride and stubbornness, made me.

I came to think he looked for glimpses of who his daughter might have become in most young women he met, and I truly believed that my wife-to-be represented what he had hoped she would have become. My aunt had been beautiful, full of life and joy, a vivacious brunette with deep dimples, cheeks that blushed easily, and an infectious smile. Lauren had some of the same qualities, mixed with a modern sensibility and a touch of the city and worldliness.

They got on thick as thieves, damn them. She pressed him for details of my childhood growing up on the farm and would wink at me with every knee-slapping recollection he shared with her. I wrecked a tractor, I wrecked a car, broke my arm climbing a huge pine in an adjacent field . . . She would laugh, touch his arm, smile at me reassuringly, and pretty much sweep him up in her all-encompassing aura of beauty and warmth. She had that way with people. We would return for a wedding on the farm the following year, and she would dance with Uncle Jack right after our first dance and her father's.

Outside of my Aunt Eunice who lived a few miles away, who I barely knew and who visited only occasionally, Uncle Jack was the only family I knew. My parents had died in a car wreck when I was four, and I had moved in with him shortly after. My first memories of the farm were from the windshield of his F-150 pickup as it pulled into the yard. I was scared beyond belief.

The huge hay barn dominated the property, and the two-story 'foursquare' farmhouse sparkled white in the sunshine. A small sauna occupied space with a small tool shed between the house and barn. Various outbuildings swept past the cattle gate into the main field beyond the barn. A huge apple orchard gleamed in the bright light of day to my left, running out to the main road.

Jack looked over at me with tears in his eyes and laid a rough hand on my shoulder.

"It is you and me now, son. I owe it to John to raise my only nephew. I don't know anything about kids, but I am hoping you find this a place to heal, to learn, work hard, and become a man."

In the intervening years, I did all those things.

I attended the Laird Township Elementary School from kindergarten through 7th grade, then junior high and high school in L'Anse, a small town on the shores of Lake Superior's Keweenaw Bay about 15 miles to the east of Alston. I played baseball, ran track, played hockey on the local rink, biked, swam, and ran through the forests of maple, poplar, and oak with my friends. Jack never missed an event. He eked out a living on the small farm, and often worked in the woods logging during the winter to supplement his income, just like the generations before him that had made Laird Township their home.

Uncle Jack encouraged reading, and had a magnificent library filled with classics and paperback westerns, thrillers, and spy novels. He had a special interest in military history, especially the American Civil War. He had an affinity for the cavalry and would regale me with tales of raids and great charges by horsemen on both sides: Jeb Stuart, Nathan Bedford Forrest, George Armstrong Custer, Joe Wheeler, John Buford . . . There were so many, each colorful in their own way.

The swayback horses in our own pasture were more pets than mighty steeds, but an old black mare named Bessie would occasionally allow me to take a leisurely ride down along the West Branch of the Sturgeon River. Any attempts at galloping or charging a neighbor's barn were met with a snort and a sharp stop. I teasingly called her "Black Bess," after the favorite mare of the Confederate Raider John Hunt Morgan. He was a dashing Southern cavalier, who had a way with the ladies, and inspired men with his lightning-like raids throughout Kentucky and surrounding states. I had absolutely no way with the "ladies" but atop this gentle mare, I did dream.

Once in a while, I would pat her on the back, and she would look back at me knowingly, her nostrils catching a scent of a past in which she could gallop for miles, strong and powerful in her youth. I would feel a ripple of muscle memory along her flank, and she would briefly trot with a few high steps, aloft on a distant memory of a time long past. She was buried on a knoll up on the upper 40 acres, with a view of the river and small valley that she loved so much, surrounded by the orchard full of apples she so loved to snack on. My usual evening walk in the fall always took me on the path near her grave, and I would stop to pat the soil and replace the apple I left each night with a fresh one.

It was the sensations of that childhood that drew me back to my hometown: the taste of a crisp, tart apple from the orchard, the cold water sipped from cupped hands on the banks of the creek, the smell of fresh-mown hay, the taste of

A&W root beer or an orange Crush after a day in the fields. The snow after a hot sauna, the feel and taste of fall — a torrent of red and old gold that filled the forest floor each September. The indescribable tang of a first kiss along the riverbank. I still took walks along those banks with my dogs, and they always lifted their heads, their ears perked up, as though they still sensed something in that spot after all those years. Perhaps like me, they could hear the laughter and in the quiet, hear a young man's prayers, supplicant in the whisper of pines.

I would repaint the old farmhouse many times, cursing while scraping the miles of clapboard siding and balancing precariously from old wooden ladders dragged out from the barn. I asked Uncle Jack many times why he stuck with white, and he would quietly remind me, as he had many times: "A man's home is a reflection of the people inside, and a window to the soul of the builder."

And so it remained white and faithfully repainted every five years. It had missed a cycle when I moved off to college, and with Jack's advancing age, it was a few extra years until I could get enough time off to come repaint it. We would sweat also in the sauna, bathing in the steam of Finnish tradition. He was unrepentant in coaxing massive rolling coils of heated mist from the Lake Superior rocks atop the wood stove, ladling cold water by the gallons from galvanized pails on the cedar benches. He always got a kick out of outlasting me in the heat. I would usually succumb as the top of my head and tips of my ears would ache in the scorching steam, and I would dash out to the changing room and race outside and to the creek to jump into the blindingly refreshing cool water. I could still taste that sweat after all these years, and feel the cool and fiery touch of the water. I saw visions in the swirling steam, my future occluded and still just distant from my outstretched palm.

Chapter 7

It was, fittingly, a night of thunder, blinding flashes of light, and the hollow boom of towering clouds above, alive in creation of a storm that set me upon the course that would change my life.

My wife and I were sitting at the kitchen table, enjoying a cold meal by candlelight since the power had gone out. During a conversation about a bathroom renovation, she caught a glimpse of our front door and screamed. My dogs raced to the front door, barking furiously.

A faceless creature stood there, framed in the glass, silhouetted in the incandescence of a flash of lightning. Rain streamed off its back and a hand reached out of the bundle of rags that constituted an overcoat. The hand tapped slightly on the glazing, and the sharp noise froze both Lauren and I for a brief moment.

I rose from the chair and reached for a flashlight, clenching it as I cautiously made my way to the door. Holding the collars of the dogs, I opened the door slightly and stared inquiringly at this strange visitor.

"May I come in?" a deep voice resonated from the blackness where a face might be. "I promise I'm not here to hurt you."

I opened the door, stepping back unconsciously, and feeling about me for another more substantial weapon. I heard the faint hiss behind me; Lauren had opened the cabinet drawer where we kept a 9-mm Smith and Wesson.

Two hands reached up and pulled back the hood of an enormous greatcoat. Rain streamed down, pooling on the tile floor. The motion revealed a huge man, framed by grey hair and thick black beard, also streaked with grey, and black eyes. Details revealed themselves as he stepped forward, hands outstretched, palms up.

"Pardon my intrusion. The rain caught me as I was walking here, and it was too late to turn back."

"Why didn't you call, or announce yourself?" I spoke, the words seeming to echo in the open door to the night.

"I don't have a phone, or a vehicle."

"Why are you here?"

"To show you something . . . may I sit?" He turned his head slightly. "Ma'am . . . you can put the gun down."

Shakily, Lauren set the gun on the counter as the man sat heavily, palms flat on the table.

"Perhaps you had best explain." My hand was gripping the Maglite tightly; I could feel the diamond pattern of the metal etching itself in my skin. But I could not say I wasn't intrigued.

He reached into the folds of a shirt and withdrew a clutched fist, which opened in front of me on the table, revealing a gleaming silver coin. "I believe it is best you sit and hear what I have to say."

The words were flat, emotionless, but something in the tone held me riveted.

He spun the coin on the table, and we watched as it landed. He considered me gravely for a few long moments, taking in the quality of his host that sat across the table from him. He looked into my eyes, and, after taking stock of me, nodded slightly and began his story.

"I was at your history presentation last Saturday at the Laird Township Hall. You spoke about your work and research trying to find out more about Henry Laird, the first township supervisor and fiery proponent of its formation. You went on to explain about some of the mysteries of his coming to America with his mother, his short time in the Union Army in 1861 at the onset of the Civil War, the gap in his history from that point until his arrival in what would become Laird Township in 1887 . . . You also explained his death of unknown causes in the wilderness north of the Township at 47 years old. He died because of this coin and its brethren, all Mexican silver."

The stranger folded his hands over his chest and smiled as I gaped at him. Total astonishment would be an understatement.

When I had moved back to Laird Township, I devoted a lot of time to researching the small town I grew up in: Alston, Michigan. Situated in southern Houghton County at the base of the Keweenaw Peninsula, which juts out into Lake Superior to form the northernmost point of the state, it was mainly in the middle of nowhere but on the way to somewhere. My uncle had said that often, and the description stuck with me.

I researched the Mineral Range Railroad that had been constructed through the township in 1900 and chronicled its short history of hauled timber, copper ore, and other items until the 1930s, when the tracks were fully pulled. I had researched the lives of David and Joseph Alston, along with August Nisula, namesakes of the two small towns which were the sparse population centers in the township. I had recently held the second of two free local history symposiums where I showed historic pictures I had digitized, and shared information on my research subjects in the area. I looked inquiringly at our guest. "I don't remember you at either presentation."

He chuckled and stood up from the table, and took off his greatcoat, which was somehow intact in spite of the ragged appearance. He then shed a number of flannel shirts, smoothed out his beard and tilted his head upward, revealing an aged and lined face that was somewhat familiar. Then I remembered. He had come in late and said little, but had gazed at me during the two hour presentation with unflagging interest and deep-set black eyes, leaving without a word to anyone.

He nodded gravely as he saw my recognition. "You were being evaluated."

Once again, astonishment flooded my features, and I tried in vain to recover. I sat down across from him.

"Perhaps you should explain."

My wife had picked up the gun again, looked at me in a pointed fashion, and replaced it in the kitchen drawer. She crossed her arms and leaned against a counter.

"You came to our attention two years or so ago, when you made inquiries in New York state about the service records of Henry Laird, ostensibly from Bethel in Sullivan County."

"But he first enlisted in May of 1861 in Elmira," I interrupted. "And was discharged 20 days later with $12.61 in pay."

He held up a hand and nodded, then continued. "Henry Laird would re-enlist in 1864 with his brother, John, in the New York 15th Heavy Artillery."

He held up a hand again as I interrupted. "Constantine, therein lies the tale."

Chapter 8

July 10, 1863 – Lexington, Indiana

General John Hunt Morgan sat erect in his saddle, keenly aware of the night about him. The warmth of the evening invited cicadas to sing as the horses approached.

"What say you, boys?" he cantered a bit out into the clearing, and let moonlight fall upon his careworn face, lined by the faintest glimmer of worry and illuminated in the glow of the summer's eve.

The three men drew up their frothing horses in the half-light glow, breathing heavily. They swung down, their boots thudding softly in the undergrowth, and walked their horses over to him. One man swept off his hat and slapped it against his thigh, lifting dust which glittered in the rays of scattered light.

"General, the militia is out in Vernon and, hell, the whole damn state. Hobson is less'n four hours behind us. We have to break camp. The Yankees have a whole brigade of cavalry after us, and more are meeting up ahead."

General Morgan absorbed the information quietly. His eyes narrowed at the news as Glencoe moved beneath him, anxious to return for another drink at the creek. The smell of fresh-mown hay was also inviting.

"Tend to your horses, they look done in." He watched in silence as the men removed their saddles and gear, and transferred them to the horses they had "appropriated" in their survey of the area.

Morgan considered his situation silently.

A dark and lean figure moved next to him, still fully upright in his saddle despite having ridden near constantly for many days and barely rested.

"Basil, we have to peel off the wagons." Morgan spoke in a low voice to his second-in-command and brother-in-law. Basil Duke sat in quiet silence as he considered the thought, his angular face and strong jaw line inscrutable in the partial light.

"All of them?"

"Yes, they will not keep up, we have to move more quickly than we are, and they are too heavily loaded. We and the South cannot afford for them to fall into Union hands."

"Bragg is going to kill you for this, John." Basil spoke of General Braxton Bragg, who had authorized a raid by Morgan's cavalry command of over 1,200 troopers but had explicitly forbade crossing the Ohio River out of Kentucky. Morgan had moved across Kentucky, actually taking 2,460 men, and, after a number of skirmishes, arrived at the Ohio at Brandenburg, commandeering two riverboats, the Alice Dean and John D. Macombs. Now with his men across southern Indiana, he set out to sweep around the Union stronghold of

Cincinnati. Union militias were rising up in Indiana, and along their intended route through southern Ohio. Union cavalry was massing and moving upon them as well.

"Basil, we are going to have to keep moving, stay north of the Yankees, come back down to the Ohio, and try to find a ford," General Morgan continued. "We are not going to make it across the state and deliver the wagons."

"Damn, I know," Basil looked across the rising mist of the cool night air and could still detect the glint of determined amusement and a belief in destiny in Morgan's eye.

"You know why we had to try," Morgan spoke softly.

Basil reined his horse away from Morgan, and his horse stepped away into the night. A soft voice carried to Morgan in the clarity of night: "I know."

Chapter 9

"My name is Simon Kyle, and we have protected this secret for generations, Constantine."

Our nighttime visitor regarded me from below heavy-lidded eyes which sat like embers in a dying fire. He spread his palms on the tabletop, the tips of his fingers moving nearly imperceptibly around the coin centered between his hands.

"Many men have died to protect this secret of the provenance of this coin and its brethren," he continued. "Many men, including the first supervisor of Laird Township." He avoided my startled stare and my wife's gasp.

"Constantine, please relate your known background of Henry Laird's life. I will pick up the threads and complete what I know of his service to our country and his death."

I leaned back, astonished. Taking a deep breath, I ran my own fingers over my scalp, calmed myself, and related what I knew.

"It really is quite a tale . . . Henry Laird came to the United States with his mother somewhere around 1847, with his brother John and sister Jane. Ship manifests are vague, but his mother, also named Jane, appeared to be travelling alone, or perhaps with her parents. Once disembarking at New York

City, it appears she took a position with the Benjamin Cross family on a farm in New York as a housekeeper or maid.

"Henry would enlist in the Union Army in May of 1861 in Elmira, New York, only to be discharged 21 days later with the sum of $12.61 in back pay. He was 16 years old, an age where recruits served as camp runners, drummer boys, or tended to horses. These recruits often invalided out or were dismissed for a variety of reasons.

"Henry Laird would reappear in the Union ranks in 1864, enlisting with his brother John in Bethel, New York. He was then 19 and John was 21. It's inexplicable why he would wait so long to re-enlist, and why his brother would wait until 1864 to join at 21 years old. They served in the 15th New York Heavy Artillery regiment, where John would be captured, and Henry wounded. Henry would be discharged from the army in 1865 from a Union hospital in Maryland.

"It was hard to trace Henry's movements from the Civil War into the 1870s, but he would appear in Baraga, Michigan in the 1880s, working as a laborer. Here he developed a relationship with a group of homesteaders in an area 14 miles west of Baraga, in a district known as Silver. He, along with these farmers, became an ardent proponent for the development of a new township in southern Houghton County. Laird Township came to be in 1887, breaking out of Portage Township and settling tax rolls with Houghton County. Henry Laird was elected to be the first township supervisor. It struck me as ironic that after fighting in a massive conflict over secession, he would for all intents engage in it himself. One record described him as a fiery orator.

"Interestingly, he did not purchase a homestead in the township until 1889, at the corner of what would become South Laird and the Ontonagon-Baraga stagecoach road. It was 78 acres. He would inexplicably sell his property in 1891 in three parcels, one of which he deeded to the township to become a site for a school. He then moved to Baraga and took up work as a timber cruiser in late 1891.

"In July of 1892, his body was found after a long search in the forests northwest of Baraga. He was 47 years old and known to be in excellent health. His body was found by two men who fashioned a raft to float his body down the Otter River. A newspaper report indicated that the body was to be transported to the county seat in Houghton for an autopsy, although there is no evidence that this was ever done.

"A researcher friend of mine found a Probate Court record dealing with his effects. His brother John would come to claim his possessions, which amounted to $97, half of which went to the lawyer and his court. There was no trace of the money gained from the sale of his property the previous fall."

I took a breath as Lauren placed glasses of ice water on the table for me and our guest, who leveled his eyes at me and gestured slightly to encourage the completion of my story. It was an old-fashioned gesture, with a forefinger etching a small arch in the space between us.

"It is here his story became strange," I continued.

Simon smiled without showing his teeth, and the act did not touch his eyes.

"He had a headstone erected in what is now the Evergreen Cemetery in L'Anse, four miles around the head of Keweenaw Bay. There was no cemetery in Alston or Laird Township at that time, but it's strange that he would be buried there and not in Baraga or Houghton. Even more strangely, he was buried with what appears to be a really nice tombstone, not the typical Civil War headstones commissioned and produced en masse by the veteran's organizations that existed after the war."

I paused, knowing the next riddle in my narrative might well be answered by this stranger at my kitchen table. "But the inscription indicates the 35th New York, which was the infantry regiment he was discharged from after 21 days in 1861. There's no mention of his later service. Even stranger, Henry Laird was not listed on the 1890 Veteran's census rolls for Laird Township. In fact, his closest neighbor in the township was a decorated trooper of the Pennsylvania Veteran Volunteers. His name was James Kyle, and he died after Henry. They're buried beside each other with identical headstones."

I paused, looking across at our guest expectantly. He gave no sign of interrupting, so I completed my narrative. His visage had gone from a cat about to pounce to an aloof, almost predatory gaze. They had taken on a flinty aspect, colored with flecks of gold. I was now reminded of the eyes of a hawk, perched high above the forest floor, watching a rabbit.

Lauren was brewing coffee now, her gaze not leaving our visitor, surely as entranced as I was.

"Surely his own brother, who had enlisted and served with him, would've gotten his regiment correct," I continued. "And also, why was he not getting a pension? Confoundingly, a search of veteran's rolls for both North and South from the Civil War recounts the service of 12 Henry Lairds, six for each side."

My guest interrupted softly. "Where was your Henry discharged following his wound recovery?"

"Point Lookout, Maryland. There was a huge Union hospital there."

My guest tilted back in his seat, and seemingly regarded me from a lofty height before leaning forward and speaking in a soft and firm voice. "It was also a huge Confederate prisoner-of-war camp."

I met his level gaze and found no sign of deceit or misdirection. The information was matter-of-fact, but heavy with promise and a sense of foreboding.

"Where else did you find Confederate Henry Lairds?"

"I found one had done time at Camp Randall near Madison, Wisconsin," I said. "His regiment was surrendered after a brutal battle at Island Number 10 near New Madrid on the Mississippi."

"And how did you reconcile that information in the search for 'your' Henry Laird?"

"I found it interesting that there was a Henry Laird in what was probably the closest prisoner-of-war camp to Upper Michigan."

"Did you also find it interesting that all Confederate Henry Lairds had done time in these camps?"

"I did. I've even joked that Henry wasn't even buried in Evergreen Cemetery — that there's Confederate gold buried in his grave instead."

"You indicated in your presentation that you and another gentleman had engaged a Ground Penetrating Radar class from Michigan Tech University to survey the cemetery plots."

My mouth was dry now; I took another long drink of water. "Yes. Results were inconclusive, there was something six feet down, but was so close to Kyle's grave, it appeared as one mass on the radar screen. Looking at the results, I almost felt that both graves were dug at the same time, and both bodies laid to rest side by side. I got everyone's attention by conjecturing there was actually Confederate gold buried instead of Henry and James's bodies."

There again was the smile. "They were dug at the same time," he said. "And our story does involve Confederate treasure."

Lauren had joined us at the table at this point. I glanced over. To say she "sat" was too general. She always seemed to levitate and glide into position, such was her manner. She now got up in a movement of equal grace, crossed to a shelf above the sink, and returned with a bottle of Elijah Craig 12-year Barrel Proof Kentucky Straight Bourbon and three glasses.

Pouring two fingers in each glass, she wordlessly downed her own.

Simon gazed speculatively at the bourbon. He ran one finger around the rim of his glass, lifted the glass in the dim light. He took a sip. "You have no idea of how closely-related bourbon is to the characters in our story." He took another small sip and nodded appreciatively. "Henry did in fact enlist in 1861, and during training, he took up acquaintance with a certain gentleman who had connections with a Mr. Allan Pinkerton."

It was my turn to down my glass, and I reached for the bottle Lauren had brought to the table. I held up a hand, finished two more fingers' worth, and sighed. I knew who Mr. Pinkerton was. Damn. I could hear the click as tiles slid into place in my mind. Like Pinkerton, Henry was born in Scotland and was also orphaned. Allan immigrated to Northern Illinois in 1842, where he was active in the Abolitionist movement. A story had him finding some counterfeiters in the woods near his home and contacting local authorities after observing them. He would become the first police detective in Chicago in 1849. He formed the North-Western Police Agency in 1850, which ultimately became the Pinkerton National Detective Agency, arguably the most famous detective agency in the United States, with a name still resonating today. Their slogan was "We Never Sleep," their logo was a wide-open eye.

Pinkerton would solve a number of train robberies in the 1850s, where he would meet a lawyer for the Illinois Central Railroad named Abraham Lincoln. He'd attend abolitionist meetings in Chicago with John Brown and Frederick Douglas. He, along with others, would help purchase supplies for John Brown, who would later lead a raid on the Federal arsenal at Harpers Ferry. John Brown was hanged by troops led by a Federal officer with the given name of Robert E. Lee. The Raid, followed by Brown's death, presaged the conflagration which would engulf the country less than two years later.

In 1861, Pinkerton was the head of the Union Intelligence Service, and also foiled an assassination attempt on the life of the President of the United States, Abraham Lincoln. Pinkerton's agents worked throughout the war, gathering intelligence for the Union War effort, often masquerading as Confederate soldiers or sympathizers. Allan used the alias Major E.J. Allen, a Confederate officer, undertaking intelligence missions on many occasions. He worked throughout the South in 1861, gathering information on fortifications and military strength. His intelligence service went on to become the foundation for the United States Secret Service.

The tiles kept clicking and dropping into place. "Are you suggesting that Henry Laird was an agent for Allan Pinkerton?" I asked.

"I am not suggesting at all," said Simon. "I am telling you that he was."

I stared at him. The tiles in my mind that had clicked into place started forming into machinery: spinning, whirring, and taking on life. My God . . .

Chapter 10

"Allan was actively recruiting in early 1861 at the onset of the war. He, along with many others, knew that the war was not going to end quickly," Simon began. "The fiasco at Bull Run, or as the South called it, Manassas, proved that. He needed agents that were young, unattached, and eager to serve the Union. With Scottish immigrants scattered through the United States, young Henry's slight Scottish accent would not stand out in the South. He was a prime candidate for Pinkerton's Secret Service. He was given a Union Army discharge, ostensibly to aid in his effort to appear as a disgruntled Federal army washout in his travels throughout the US.

"He travelled through the South and got "caught" up in a few recruiting efforts. He served in a very dangerous capacity, and got caught in a number of battles, most notably at New Madrid. He found opportunity to "surrender" and get taken prisoner. Allan found use for him also in Confederate POW camps, collecting information on unit strength, news from Richmond, and other information.

"Henry became a specialist in hunting down stolen payrolls, both North and South. He traced counterfeiting efforts in the south to reproduce Federal currency, and also advised on the production of counterfeit Southern currency in the North, an attempt to flood the South and undermine the value of their dollars. That proved to be unnecessary, as inflation and lack of specie backing did that anyway."

"How do you know all this?" I asked.

Again, that enigmatic smile. It tugged at the corners of his mouth, and drew at the lines around his face, but still did not touch his eyes.

"That is a tale for another day, a long one, and a journey of great time and distance." Simon's hands fell flat to the table, and he pushed himself up slowly, with effort in the lifting. "I see it's very late. I should be heading home."

"I will give you a ride," I offered.

"No, I prefer to walk. The rain and the night air do me well."

"Please, can we meet again tomorrow to discuss this more?"

"Of course, we have much to discuss, and still more for me to uncover for you. I'll call on you tomorrow. Keep the coin for now as a token of my sincerity."

He left then, bundling back up in the great overcoat. He offered apologies for the pool of water on our linoleum floor and left with a flashlight we insisted he carry with him.

I leaned against a post on the front porch of our house, listening to his footsteps down the drive, carried to me on the vagrant breeze lingering after the storm. The creak of the old wooden swing to my left lent a melancholy note upon this song of night. I lifted a hand to caress a fluted groove along the post, catching a paint chip in my palm. The old house was due for another paint job.

I mindfully held the white chip between my thumb and forefinger, pondering the astonishing news of the last hour in our kitchen.

Lauren came from behind, curled one arm around me, and put her head on my shoulder. The she turned to go into the house and I followed, but glanced over my shoulder, still thinking I should grab the old Ford truck and go after him.

Chapter 11

I always get up early but was nonetheless startled by the knock on the front door the next morning. Sunlight was just starting to stream into the yellow kitchen. I answered the door and was taken aback to find a Houghton County Sheriff's deputy standing there, haloed in the golden light of a morning sunrise.

"Good morning?" I asked.

The deputy was in her mid-thirties, pretty and athletic, of medium height with dark hair worn short.

"Did you have any visitors last night?" The voice surprised me with its soft undertones. A restless and cutting chill ran through me, an icy finger that moved down my arms.

"Yes," I said. "We could start with good morning."

She scowled at my comment. "Could you describe them?"

"Larger build, stocky, black unkempt hair, streaked with grey. Why do you ask? Did something happen?"

"Why would you ask if something happened? Do you know something?" She almost spat out the words. "Houghton County's finest usually do not appear at your front door on a beautiful morning without cause. What happened?"

She relaxed visibly and asked if she could come in. She gestured at another male deputy standing next to the car.

"He can come in too," I said.

Inside, I poured three cups of coffee.

"So what happened to him?"

She glanced at the floor, seemingly studying the patterns of blue and grey in the linoleum and then looked up, fixing her attention squarely on me. She spoke quietly.

"He was found dead on the side of the road just around the corner from your place here."

I know my face turned ashen. I was truly shocked. I was even more shocked they were here and somehow connected him to me. I had nothing to say, I moved my gaze up to the ceiling and then closed my eyes. A few plaster cracks had opened up again, straining against decades of paint of varying colors. When I opened my eyes and returned my focus to her, she was studying me intently. She wanted a response. I could see that in the tightly drawn corners of her eyes, the hard line of her mouth.

"I met him for the first time last night. He showed up to visit and introduce himself. His name was Simon." She kept her gaze fixed on me. "I am sorry, what was your name again?"

"My name is Anderson." She hesitated, and then added. "Isabella. Bella."

"Bella, he visited for an hour or so, and then left here to walk home."

"Are you aware he lives three miles away?" she asked.

"Do you know where he lives? What did he visit with you about?" Rapid fire, her mind was racing quickly; she had some training for these situations. She even blinked as she processed questions and my reactions simultaneously.

"Bella, last night was the first we spoke."

"Let's also stick with Officer Anderson," she said. "What did you talk about? Why was he here?"

"He wanted to discuss some of my research on Laird Township."

"What specifically?"

I mentally stiffened and recoiled. "My history presentations and seminars."

She looked around the kitchen at my neat piles of research documents, folders. and associated detritus of a writer without an official office. Dark coffee rings were present on some on sheets of paper. "I understand you have written some books?"

"Yes, local history and people." I coughed slightly. "Should I contact a lawyer?" I looked away.

She seized on that. "Why, did you do something? What do you know about Simon?"

"No, I did nothing. But why does this feel like an interrogation?"

Her partner rose from the table, one hand hanging loosely near his side. A gun sat menacingly inches from his palm.

I stood up and walked to the door, then gestured outside.

I could feel the progression of heat building up in my face. But now I was curious. "Can you show me where he was found? Did he have a heart attack? Stroke?"

"Let's go for a ride." Officer Anderson got up and adjusted her gun belt. It seemed like an odd movement, but I guess all officers did that.

"I would rather walk," I said. "Walk with me."

The somber nature of our journey contrasted with the beauty of the morning. Sparrows sang from the trees along the road, and the morning light filtered through the forest to our left as we walked in silence.

The area around the body was crudely cordoned off. He lay on his back, a misshapen husk devoid of the vital vapor of life. He lay on the edge of the gravel road, with the lower half of his body in the grass along the shoulder, his feet in a small ditch. He was hatless, and his arms were outstretched, and his face had been mercifully covered by a small blanket, presumably provided by a first responder or the deputies.

The male deputy spoke for the first time. "It looks like a hit and run. The autopsy will reveal if there were any other injuries prior to the vehicle hitting him." His hardened face softened briefly while speaking, then resumed its glacial countenance.

"It had to be close to 10:30 or 11:00 when he left," I said. "Did you find a flashlight? I gave him one for his walk home."

Officer Anderson gave me a quizzical look. "No, we haven't found anything not on his person. I don't want you getting close to this crime scene, please go back."

I stopped ten feet away. "This is the only road off my property — can you check tire tracks or something?"

She averted her gaze from me, and stiffly nodded.

"My God. Is that him?"

I turned to see Lauren standing behind us. She reached for

me, a bit unsteady on her feet.

"Did either of you leave your house with a vehicle after he left?" Officer Anderson asked.

"No, I don't go into work until this afternoon," Lauren responded.

Mrs. Deputy turned to me now. "And you?"

"I freelance from home, so no, neither of us has left since he did last night."

Both deputies gave me a half-derisive look, mixed with a hint of amusement and a slight touch of disbelief. I had seen the look before. This was still a blue-collar area, where people are expected to get up early, head to work, work hard, and be home for supper. Then they are often expected to work in the evening in their yards, or on their farms, or work a side job. At least, it was that way when I was growing up. Perceptions and realities were changing, but slowly.

"I am a writer." My add-on felt awkward and miss-timed. I got the same look.

"Go home," said Officer Anderson. "Both of you."

Chapter 12

The sun was brutally hot. Zeke worked in silence, assigned to stack lumber as it came out of the mill. The sawdust swirled in a choking cloud. He stopped to lift a handkerchief up to his face, and a sudden, powerful blow leveled him into the pile of sawdust beneath him. He put a hand to the back of his head, put his hat back on, and resumed working, pulling another plank off the rollers.

Danny laughed behind him and said mockingly: "Don't let me catch you shirking again — you take a break when I say." He crossed his arms and cast his half-lidded glance through his small round eyes.

"How about facing a man?" asked Zeke. "Is that the way you win fights, hitting people from behind?"

The voice whipped across the heavy air, striking Danny physically. He shook his shaggy head as if he couldn't believe what he heard. "I think it is time for a whipping, before I fire you." He rolled his heavy shoulders, twisted his neck in a half-circle, and started rolling up his sleeves.

"Well, alright, but if I whip you," said Zeke. "I get double pay for the day, and so does every man on this shift. Deal?"

Danny nodded and stepped forward, immediately punching from chest level. Zeke ducked the blow, but it glanced off his left shoulder. Danny had power.

Zeke planted his left leg, and punched from waist level, catching the bigger man in the wind. A sharp intake of breath and a wheeze greeted him. Danny had relied on his size and intimidation too long. Now he needed to sharpen up.

Danny closed in on the smaller man, dropping blows into the small semi-circle of space between them. Zeke blocked most with his forearms and struck wickedly into the nose of the big man. Blood dripped from the broken nose, and Danny wiped it away casually, with a cunning look that spread over his face. Taking another blow up high, he came up with a slab of wood and swung it with both hands into the shoulder his opponent.

Zeke dropped to the sawdust-covered yard, stinging from the force of the blow.

Danny dropped the slab, advancing now on his wounded prey, anxious to satiate his need to belittle and destroy. Zeke parried a few ineffectual blows, drawing away to bide time, his arm numbing up. He had to finish this quickly. He let himself be drawn in close, which Danny seized upon, grabbing him around the shoulders, squeezing tightly, letting his muscles constrict, and intending to suffocate.

Zeke could hear the shouted encouragement from the workers that surrounded them — A dozen or so were drawn the spectacle. Many of them had felt the lash of Danny's treatment and anxiously watched the fight unfold before them.

They winced as Danny started to crush his opponent.

Zeke could feel the air escaping him, and he was unable to draw additional breaths, further choked by the whirl of dust around them.

Sensing victory, Danny leaned in with a leer.

A head butt caught him off-guard, the second impacted a cheekbone. Zeke fell loose, landing catlike on his feet, drawing breath with one hand on the ground, holding that stance momentarily as Danny pawed at his wounded face.

Danny roared and charged, stomping a heavy boot at Zeke and falling to the ground as it missed. Zeke fell upon him with lightning quick blows into his face. Danny flailed like a wounded bear, flipping Zeke off into an adjacent lumber pile. Zeke's own head rang with the blow.

They stepped in together, traded blow for blow, and expended their fury upon one another. Heavy blows struck flesh with hollow sounds that echoed across the yard. A shot rang out, and the onlookers turned to see Hank Glasset striding across the yard, a smoking pistol in his hand pointed skyward.

Danny and Zeke were still squaring off, ignoring Hank's shouts. Danny swung out in a wide arc, intending a finishing blow. Zeke stepped into the rush of wind, striking deep into the stomach of the big man, feeling the wind expel from the body. Danny was half-slumped now, and Zeke swung upward with a double strike to the man's chin, his head snapping back and his unconscious body falling like a tree.

The yard was silent. Hank had stopped ten feet away. "Draw your pay and get off my land."

"Danny promised everyone a double share for day shift if I won," Zeke said. "I did, so pay them too."

"He doesn't run this mill. I do."

A small dark man with a thick mustache yelled out: "I seen it. Danny hit him from behind. This man had no choice."

Others echoed the sentiment; hands were raised, anxious to insert their eyewitness accounts. Ignoring Hank, Zeke walked over to a barrel on the edge of the yard, plunged his hands into the water, and cupped handfuls onto his face, running his fingers through his black hair. He took up a bucket from the ground and filled it, then silently walked back and threw it on to the fallen form of Danny.

Danny gasped and shook his head, rolling over. As his vision cleared, he pointed a finger at Zeke.

"It was fair," he said. "But you have two minutes to get off this property." He looked over at Hank. "He was shirking'"

Hank was walking away. "I doubt it." He called over his shoulder.

Hands were clapping Zeke on the back, enthusiastic in their praise. The giant had been felled and humbled. Zeke saw smiles all around him.

"We are all buying a round at Willette's after work for you!"

He couldn't make out who said that, but there was enthusiastic nodding from the entire assembled group. They were all similarly-dressed in their open-collared shirts, suspenders, and slouch caps. A few wore bandanas against the dust.

Another man put his arm around his shoulder and whispered. "After you have those drinks, you should come to Felix's place, and get some relaxation for those tired muscles." The comment slid out, sly and rank in the open air.

"Felix's?" Zeke looked at him from his left eye. The right was swelling up. "Women?"

"Better yet, girls. You will like them, young and pretty. They have had the feisty taken out of them. Just ignore the chains and have some fun. Cost you not even today's pay." The dark little man leered through tobacco-stained lips, eagerly rubbing his mustache, excited to share his illicit news with this hero of the moment "Take the northeast trail of the site, follow the creek for a half-mile, and come up into the gully at the gate. Tell 'em Jenks sent ya."

Zeke nodded grimly, turning away to hide the smoldering in his eyes. The beating had yielded its intended effect. He straightened, looking over at Danny.

Danny, looking around with eyes of hatred at the crowd drifting away, returned the gaze once the last of the onlookers fell away and returned to their work. As the buzzsaw shriek resumed, and shouts of men carried across the yard, Zeke lifted a hand to the brim of his hat, pulling it down slightly, saluting the giant.

Danny dipped his head slightly in acknowledgement, and walked away into the sun-filtered yard.

Chapter 13

Lauren and I made an appearance at the Houghton County Sheriff's office the following day, giving formal depositions about the night Simon died. We did not share every detail on Henry Laird, but as the coin might be a clue, we did describe it to the recording officer.

"Why did he show you a coin?" The officer was a thickset man with closely-cropped black hair. With reading glasses balanced on his nose, he appeared to be almost scholarly, with an air of resignation.

"He had found it and thought I might know something about where it came from, as a historian. It was a Mexican coin from the 1860s." I described it as best I could, quick to note it was silver, and taking any possible motive I might have out of the equation.

"Don't plan on leaving the county any time soon. We may want to talk again." The familiar female voice was behind me. We turned to face Officer Anderson. "I mean it, too. Don't take any trips."

She didn't put her thumbs into her gun belt, but the aura of threat was there nonetheless. We left, exiting out into the summer sunshine and a freshening breeze. I felt guilty breathing it, knowing Simon would no longer. I was sure he had been murdered, but I couldn't fathom a motive.

These events haunted me, and the mystery drew me back to my research. The route to his home on Cemetery Road had been cordoned off, supposedly due to the washout of a culvert, so a trip to his home proved problematic. I did take a hike through the woods due south of M-38 to his property, but numerous postings and miscellaneous threats to trespassers gave me pause. I had proceeded to the edge of his yard to find the site wrapped with yellow police tape. A small sign planted on the sparse grass gave notice to surveillance cameras.

Days went by, Lauren accepted a job at Michigan Tech's library, and I returned to my writing. I wrote a piece about Simon for Michigan History Quarterly, with vague details about an interest in history and the possibility of literary and historical treasure laying about the township. I shared the mystery of the life of Henry Laird, leaving out the startling revelation of his service as a Pinkerton. The editor had called and pressed me for details, catching the scent of a larger story, and I demurred. Simon had possibly died for his knowledge. Unease lingered in our home, and Lauren and I danced around the topic when we met briefly every night for supper. We stuck to mundane details about our days and took long evening walks with the dogs. The road was dusty during mid-summer, but thankfully, traffic was light.

One evening, the oppressive heat made us cut our normal four-mile walk down to two. As we made our way home, we heard a terrific roar and the sound off engines racing back towards our house. Lauren gasped and pointed as we saw a heavy plume of black smoke pour into the sky above the tree line separating us from the property. We broke into a run as inky black columns of stained the darkening skies, and the orange-crested clouds of the horizon soon became obscured with the flames of nightmares.

Lauren was frantically trying to dial her phone while running. We notoriously had no signal near the farm. We rounded the corner into horror. Grey and Satch were barking furiously at the barn, which was engulfed in an inferno. Lauren gasped, running for her car to pull the Nissan out of the way. I ran to the house to call 911. There was no tone. I grabbed my charging cell phone and ran upstairs, hoping to get a few bars of signal. I heard a faint voice pick up, and I yelled directions and our fire number, praying they would hear. The line went dead and I leaped off the upper porch, rolling to a stop in the grass of the front yard. I ran over to the faucet on the exterior wall and started rolling out the garden hose. I knew it was futile, but could do nothing else.

I heard Lauren scream and point. Following her outstretched finger, I could barely make out the words spray painted on the massive barn door, so thick was the dark curling smoke: "Shut up, Professor. Last warning."

I stood, stunned, momentarily freezing before watching the flames consume the door in its entirety. I pointed the feeble stream of water at the flames, sweeping the front of the barn, before I heard an unearthly screeching. I looked up in horror to see the roof buckling and grinding against the destructive maw of the fire. Lauren screamed again, and I turned to run.

The impact of the collapse tore the wind from me and propelled me into the gravel driveway. I impacted the sharp gravel, rolling up to catch the last lingering glance of a fallen dream. The monolith, which had stood for over 80 years, fell into a shower of raging crimson and a crescendo of thunder. The reverberations of collapse echoed throughout the fields and forest surrounding us.

We stared, transfixed by the howling nightmare, covered in ash and disbelief. Lauren clung to me. The dogs had come running to us. I thought of the barn cats, and prayed they made it out. We heard the echoes of the sirens carry across the fields, as three fire departments were guided by the tower of black above us, screening the sun and beckoning oblivion.

***

Lauren sat shivering on the couch, wrapped in a blanket despite the heat of the night and smoldering ruins outside. She refused to take a shower, and rocked back and forth, inconsolable in what I thought was her grief.

I quietly let the fire chiefs know what had happened. No, we had no idea why it went up. Yes, we had heard the whine of vehicle engines. Yes, we had found freshly rutted trails from off-road vehicles leaving our yard to the south. Yes, we think someone set it. I ignored the glares from fire-fighters; I supposed Simon's fate was well-known in Alston by this point. Many were suspicious, and I couldn't also shake the feeling that some of our arsonists had returned to help fight the fire.

When everyone had left, Lauren spoke quietly in the unearthly silence.

"Why didn't you tell them about the message?"

I struggled with the words, I looked down at my blackened hands, forearms singed and starting to blister. "I couldn't."

She stared at me. "Why?"

"The message was personal. They would have discounted it anyway."

Lauren did not move or speak for a long minute. "I've had enough. We have had enough. We need to move away from here, at least for a while. I can take the isolation, but not the danger."

I looked at her with what I knew were red-rimmed eyes, staring out from the hollow depths of the horror we had just observed. Now, more than ever, I needed to know why. Why was someone killed, why were we threatened?

"Lauren, I can't run now. This is my home! This is my land. If we left now, it would be giving in to threats, intimidation!" I stood, shaking in my rage, venting it on the night around me, trying to deflect my shock and anger away from her. "I have to find out who did this."

"If I mean anything to you, you will leave with me. These are just things. I mean it. This is it!"

I was stunned. "We need sleep. A shower, food. Let's talk later. Please."

"Conn, you don't understand, I was with you in rehab, the surgeries. I have lived with our pain already."

"Understand what? That I am being threatened? That you want me to cower and run?" My rage boiled over, and I jabbed a finger at her. "What kind of a man do you think you married?"

She was silent, unrepentant in my attempt at righteous anger.

"I am planning on leaving. Alone. I need room to breathe. I don't care if you come. You should be concerned about what is most important to you." She spoke more quietly; I had to strain to hear her. Outside, I heard a snap and a pop. "I didn't want to marry a martyr. I lived with that possibility already."

I stood helpless in the kitchen. She had bowed her head, folded into herself and the dark blue quilt wrapped around her. She had stopped rocking, and pulled her feet up onto the couch, curling into a fetal position, signaling that the conversation was over. I lifted my hands, and she looked at me with tears in her eyes, but she did not reach out.

I stood at the picture window, looking eastward to the strains of sunrise. Tendrils of red light reached upward, drawing chords of silence upon the strings of the morning. A new day was dawning, with the old mantra "red skies in morning, sailors take warning" portending the coming storm. I stood, buffeted by the emotion confined in the room, my gaze riveted on the red-tinged ruins of my grandfather's dream, torn by a past and my pride.

I went upstairs, stripping my clothes and stepping into the shower. I bowed my head into the stream of water, not moving until the hot water ran out. I then let the cold water pound away at the heat pouring off me: mentally and physically. The caged tension poured out, and I slammed my forearm into the tile walls of the shower, helpless in the sweep of events of the day.

Oblivion overtook me as I fell to the bed. The sweet tang of madness melted away with the onrushing dark. I heard Lauren whisper softly.

"I will try to stay, try to understand . . . " Her voice trailed off.

We would start again in the morning. I reached out to her, but she rolled away from me.

I barely slept. It was a night of restless nightmares, both real and imagined. I finally got out of bed at 5: 00 a.m. I walked out onto the porch, the smell of destruction and ash-tinged air carried through the property. I stood, bereft in the maelstrom of loss. I sat in the porch swing, unmoving.

I finally stood and walked down the steps. I stopped and reached down for one of my aunt's roses, blooming gracefully in the midst of desolation. I stooped and breathed deeply, the scent was strong enough to overcome the bitter and acrid air surrounding me. This was her home, too. I couldn't leave.

I looked toward the road, dropped my eyes and slowly turned, my world framed by new realities and the resounding echo of resolution. It was truly a new day. Somehow I would make it through and reclaim what was now, at least temporarily, a lost life.

Chapter 14

The summer rushed onward. We engaged a local builder and childhood friend, Davey Johnson, to rebuild the barn, and I was able to work with the crews on and off. We settled with the insurance company for a sum large enough to build a pole building on roughly the same footprint of the old structure.

Lauren and I kept a silent emotional distance between us. I stayed up late many nights, typing away on my computer in the kitchen, while she sequestered herself in the bedroom upstairs. We took far fewer walks, and I was often exhausted from working with the builders.

My research into local records at the county courthouses led me to find some unusual investments from the late 1860s and early 1870s by a Wesley family in the area, namely some mining ventures in Rockland and a lumber mill in Baraga. There were also significant tracts of land purchased, along with mineral rights. These struck me as unusual, given the national economic depression of 1873 in the United States during the administration of Ulysses S. Grant. A genealogy check interestingly led to a Moore family and Moore Industries, which was a major trucking, logging, and land development company in Michigan and Wisconsin. I found a filing for a legal name change by four members of the family in 1890, and the Wesley name seemed to disappear from deeds, annual corporate filings, and stockholder reports thereafter.

In late July, we had celebrated the completion of the barn by heading to Mili's, a restaurant on the backroads to Houghton. Lauren and I had both ordered the roast beef special, and we had a hard time holding eye contact with one another. She continued to hold resentment over my refusal to leave town, and the truth lay smoldering between us even in the heavy air of the restaurant.

I lifted a glass of water. "A toast to better days ahead, and a fresh start."

She looked at me, with an ironic glint in her eye, and it appeared to come from a place of derision, rather than amusement. "I want a new start somewhere other than here." Her words fell flat and toneless on the table.

I reached out a hand for hers, and she pulled away.

"I was going through some of your paperwork when you were in the sauna last night. You aren't letting any of this go, are you?" As her voice rose, others around us in the restaurant looked away uncomfortably. "You haven't stopped digging. You are obsessed with Henry Laird, the damned treasure, and sticking your nose where you were warned not to!"

She was trembling, the fear carried in her voice through her anger. I looked down at my laced hands. She wasn't done.

"Yesterday, two men showed up at the house when you were in Baraga, asking about you and your whereabouts and asked if you had any spiral bound notebooks. They asked to come in, and I told them you would be home later. I am scared, Conn."

"Were they law enforcement?" I was angry now she hadn't mentioned it last night, but then again, I did get home after midnight. "What were they driving? How were they dressed?"

She reached in her purse and handed me a card. National Trucking, a subsidiary of Moore Industries. No names. I looked up, and she was still, hands clasped in front of her, trying to contain her emotion.

An older gentleman and his wife looked over with pity and gave me hard glances. I stood up, and reached out a hand for her, but she refused to stand. I stood helplessly, finally turning to walk towards the door. A voice caught me as I reached for the entry door handle.

"Keep walking, hotshot. No way to treat a lady."

"Excuse me?" Four men were at a corner table, two dressed in button down shirts with open ties, the others wore denim shirts with sleeves rolled up. The mouthy gentleman had a thick beard. He adjusted the brim of his Mack Truck baseball cap and rose from the wooden chair.

"There's the door, boy."

Two of his companions laughed, one regarded me from behind a water glass, seemingly monitoring the situation. My retort of "Watch your language, there are kids present" didn't seem to go over too well.

I turned the door handle, and stepped out wordlessly, wondering how much of the conversation was heard in the restaurant. Too much.

I stood on the porch, next to a signboard that proclaimed "Home Cooking," and I heard the door open. The bearded man stepped out, along with two of his buddies. I stepped off the porch and spun on the gravel. They moved down the steps and spread out in a semi-circle. My new friend grinned. He rubbed a thumb across his beard and turned his head to spit ceremoniously.

All three moved in at once, I crouched and stepped off from a planted leg, striking for the mouth. He was surprised, seemingly expecting me to recoil. I was probably going to get my ass handed to me, so I may as well go down fighting. Blows flew from three directions. I felt the wind knocked out of me, but I landed two more shots and saw two of them go down. I fell on one knee in the gravel and was stunned by a blow to the side of my head. I shook it groggily, rolling away from the group. I stood and faced off with them again. I stepped into them again, smashing another fist into the mouth of my friend.

"Enough!"

The voice was commanding. My three attackers stopped, and our four heads turned to the porch where Lauren stood next to the fourth companion.

"Another day," he said, reaching out to Lauren and apologizing. My friend threw a finger at me. "Your day is coming." The doors slammed on two dark green extended cab pickups, and they pulled off onto the highway.

Lauren walked silently to our car, and we drove home in silence.

***

The next morning, I woke up to a note.

Conn, you know I love you. I love Alston too, but not enough to stay here and lose everything. You are single-minded in so many things, a product of your Finnish ancestry I guess. But I feel betrayed by your work and the risk you have placed on us. I have lived with that too many years, and cannot deal with the uncertainty. I am taking a sabbatical from the University to spend time with my sister in Wisconsin, and maybe a few friends. I need to get away. I just need distance, and you need to work through whatever this is. I think you need to start worrying about your future — our future — rather than the distant past that you seem to find so precious. I don't know what to do, besides giving you that space.

I gripped the tabletop with white-knuckled hands. I looked down and released my grip, seeing the fresh scrapes and abrasions from the fight the previous evening, stark in relief against the pale flesh.

Adrift in my confusion, I stepped out into the coming dawn and stared off across the fields. The morning mist seemed to close into the yard, reaching out to choke me.

Grey and Satch whined at the front door, and I stood a moment, taking in the yard alongside my personal history and what I held so dear, cursing at the circumstances and my nature that drove her away. I opened the door and the two dogs bounded down the steps, chasing away the tremors of night and following the lingering scents of a past that bound me so powerfully and painfully to this place.

***

Davey Johnson honked the horn loudly in the driveway, and I waved from the kitchen window while screwing the cap on the thermos I had just filled with coffee. I pulled on my weather-beaten Detroit Tigers cap, wiped away a tear from my cheek, slipped into a red flannel over shirt, and stepped out onto the porch of my home on a frosty October morning. Davey's Blue Chevy pickup puffed contentedly in a crook of the circular driveway. I opened the door and slid into the passenger's seat.

"Pretty nice ride, Davey," I said.

He regarded me across the center console with a grin. Davey Jones, as we have called him since elementary school, has retained a bit of the piratical look he has had for thirty years, though he has augmented his lean cheeks with permanent stubble. He grew into a six-foot-two lean and powerful man, which served him well in his chosen career as a home-builder. He pulled out onto the dirt road leading out of my property. It was only a two-mile drive to the building site. We moved in silence down the road as he worked a tobacco chew in the cheek closest to me. I commented on activity going on in the pole building along the highway M-38 as we passed, a couple of guys with trucker caps and flannel shirts were loading up a panel van. I thought I recognized the old pickup of two backwoods locals: sometimes loggers, full-time rednecks.

"Was that the Haakanen brothers? What are they doing on the township treasurer's place?"

Davey shrugged and glanced at me out of the corner of his eye. "Why the hell should you care? I think you should mind your own business."

Taken aback, I let that slide, anxious to get to work and warm up on this cold morning. I had pulled back from writing these days, concentrating more on research. I had taken the job with Davey to earn some extra cash going into the winter.

We pulled up to the property where he was framing a home. It was going to be a pretty straightforward one-story ranch house with a full basement. The owners were a married couple who were travelling nurses seeking some roots and stability. Davey really wanted to get it closed in before snowfall. We strapped on our tool belts, and I adjusted the suspenders on mine to accommodate the extra layers I had on. Our breath steamed in the air around us, and the expanse of white covering the ground made footing a bit treacherous.

Another pickup pulled up and Zack Morris stepped out. He was a sullen, smallish man with a hooked nose and a generally sour outlook on life. He was Davey's framing partner and hardly talked to me over the last week. He chain-smoked all day long, which annoyed me to no end, but I was the temporary help, he was Davey's partner.

We had our morning coffee sitting on the first floor of the house, the walls half-framed around us. The air was still crisp and cool. I persisted in following up my previous observation. "What were the Haakanen brothers up to this morning? Looks like they were loading up some trucks when we drove by."

The ferret-faced Zack gave a sharp sideways glance to Davey and looked down at the deck and the framing nail-gun at his feet, its yellow air-hose trailing off the edge of the plywood floor to the compressor near the pickup.

"Who knows, they always got something going." He took another sip of coffee, and spat on the deck, the ever-present tobacco chew in temporary abeyance.

"We need to get back to work, we just get chilled sitting here. Conn, why don't you finish framing up the stairs down into the basement?"

I got up, stiff in the morning cold, and walked over to the opening in the floor we had cut out that morning. The two-by-twelve pine stringers were next to the opening, ready for me to lay the treads. I turned to get a set of sawhorses and felt three sharp percussive blows in my back which staggered me. I spun, stunned by sudden pain, and instinctively reached behind my back like a wounded bear, feeling for the killing arrow. Two more blows struck me in my chest, and I stared at the fathomless dark eyes of Davey, holding the framing nailer in front of him. I grasped the nails protruding from the front of my jacket, and mouthed, or rather grasped: "Why?"

"You ask too many questions, and we don't like where your research was leading you."

74

Davey half-turned as if to walk away, then violently swung a leg at me, and I fell backward into the stair opening, falling for an eternity and then slammed into a momentary oblivion.

***

I reached through the dark fog, feeling around me, the cold concrete supporting me as I tried to stand. Waves of betrayal and disbelief washed over me. I wiped blood from my face and cursed the fact that I couldn't see. I smelled smoke from a fire, and then looked up to see the spread of flames on the floor above me. The entire deck was aflame. I wiped a glove across my face, looking up, trying to find the stair opening, where a ladder was set up during framing. It was gone, and the opening in the deck had been sheathed over.

I was trapped.

I could taste the acrid drops of gasoline they must have poured on the deck above. I brushed aside the momentary desperation, gasping at the wounds from nails. They had thought me dead and were making the house my funeral pyre. I wondered why I wasn't dead, but it flashed away in my panic to escape.

Small streams of light penetrated the flames and smoke from the basement windows that were built into the foundation. Fangs of heat brushed against me while flashes of bright orange and licking flames rained from above. My jacket was on fire now. Choking on the smoke, I clawed through the heat and fumbled at a stack of 16-foot two-byfours. I lifted one, hefting it and cradling it under one arm like a battering ram, and half-stumbled, half-ran across the basement — an attempt to knock out the temporary plywood panels we had put up in the window openings.

My ram struck the opening squarely and jarred me off my feet. I fell heavily to the concrete, screaming as I landed on my damaged arm. I rose up, drunkenly, and hammered the panel again. It fell out, and a stream of fresh air flowed in, only to have its oxygen consumed and fan the flames around me. I struggled to get a few boxes of 16 penny framing nails over to the opening, to give me enough of a boost to scramble out through the opening. I screamed again as I twisted into the opening, flames lapping at the heels of my boots, my arm useless and banging painfully on the window jamb.

I collapsed on the wet dirt outside the foundation and shambled down the grassy slope to the nearby creek. I splashed into the shallow water and rolled into a small pool, steam rising from my burned clothes. I tried to maintain consciousness, fighting through waves of pain and the smoke that clawed at my throat.

A rime of ice fringed the water, and slippery copper oak leaves made navigating the banks difficult. I collapsed again with a scream, somehow soundless in the morning air. I wrenched the rags of my jacket from my shoulders and felt the sharp twinges of pain as the nails pulled free. I struggled to free the harness of my tool belt from my torso and stared at the neat row of three nails that had been hammered into the intersection of the suspender webbing as it met in a cross on my back. Miraculously, this had probably saved my life. Just enough of the nails made it through to prick my skin, there was blood tipping each. The two nails in front were low on my left side, embedded and indescribably painful. They had caught on the jamb of the window, and had torn open jagged streaks. I pulled them free, too numb to scream, and just closed my eyes at the strike of pain.

Gasping for breath, on my knees in the water, I looked back at the house, which had flames shooting up into the blue sky of the morning, the entire structure engulfed. It struck me that Davey and Zack were probably at my house, tearing it apart. Davey's last words had mentioned my research before he attempted my. . . murder.

I had to get home. I looked up the driveway, and both pickups were gone. There were no neighbors for a half-mile.

My house was through the woods, nearly three quarters of a mile along this creek that also flowed through my property. I would lose time making it up to the road, plus they might see me and finish the job they undertook. I had to try.

I struck out down the creek-bed, my run more of a knee-slamming flight of desperation, with more time face-down in the water or along the slippery banks than upright. Branches whipped my face, drawing small drops of blood. My head ached terribly — the lingering concussion and sledgehammer force of the fall had been broken by an outflung arm, which dangled uselessly by my side, its half-swinging attempt to balance my journey only a reminder of pain. Shafts of sunlight bit through the forest into the creek bed, only serving to hide branches and rocks and holes in my frantic run. I surely hit everyone.

I reached my property and stumbled into the yard. Smoke was peeling off the roof of the house, and flames were just reaching up the walls. I hit the basement patio glass shoulder-first, collapsing into a cascade of shards and acrid smoke. I stumbled up the stairs, painfully dragging myself up the steep incline. I called for Satch and Grey. I found them both at the front door, lying on the ground, legs twitching. I smashed the front door and carried them both out into the yard. I sat between them, opening their mouths and praying for a gasp of breath. Grey shuddered and his legs stretched out. I curled my hand around his mouth, cupping it into a funnel and blowing into his mouth frantically, feeling his chest move and slowly fill. I glanced over at Satch, who was breathing laboriously. I caressed his chest with one hand and stayed by their sides. Grey gasped and rolled over on his front paws, swaying his head. He crawled over to Satch and laid his head on his friend.

Satch reached up and licked the side of Grey's face. I patted them both and stumbled back up the smoldering steps, heading for my gun cabinet. It had been smashed open and emptied. I stumbled downstairs and overturned a small table near the smashed patio door, fishing out a steel-framed small suitcase. Hauling back my one good arm, I flung the case through the smashed frame out onto the deck. It hit, bounced once and rolled into the yard.

I grabbed a few photo albums and stumbled back into the basement, falling into a heap at the bottom of the stairs.

Needles of pain shot through my body, every muscle afire and screaming at me to collapse. Give in. Sleep a dreamless and endless sleep. Massive hammers pounded at my chest and fingers of flame clawed at my jeans, beasts that sensed their prey was at bay. Demons of exhaustion pressed down on my shoulders and would not allow me to rise, they whispered as the licking fire spoke in wicked tongues. I tasted the sweet kiss of death and it knew me intimately. It called with a secret and sacred code, deliciously sweet amid the pain. The dark voices grew in intensity, a chorus of screeching talons raked across my senses.

I struggled to my feet, determined to make them pay. They tried to kill me, kill my animals, burn everything I knew, and wipe me from the Earth. I had no idea why, but I would sort out vengeance once I made it outside. Lurching to the shattered glass patio door in the basement, I stumbled out into the yard, conscious of only getting the case out into the woods near the creek. I flung it into some thick tag alders and gave into oblivion, collapsing on the grass.

Chapter 15

I awoke to a bright light, painfully aware of a thousand sparks of pain throughout my body. Small explosions knifed through me at every conscious thought. I looked down through clouded vision and saw that I was in a hospital bed, my right arm in a dressing. White sheets encased my bandaged body. "Bruised" was a vast understatement of how I felt and looked. "Battered" grew closer . . . perhaps "pummeled."

I took in the smell of some kind of antiseptic and starch from the sheets. Other lingering odors floated from the far reaches of unseen adjacent spaces, human functions, and food. I was ravenously hungry. The only thing I had eaten in recent, vague memory was smoke and a few scraps of bark that whipped their way into my mouth from branches that assailed my headlong, desperate flight down the creek bed.

I saw the shadow of a figure outside the room, a vague form through the opaque glass partition. As I pondered the presence of this person, a woman entered with my friend.

"Good morning, Officer," I managed to get out.

She did not smile, only whispered something to the nurse, who left after checking a few monitors. I may have had most of my body replaced by bionic parts, such was the morass of wires and tubes radiating outward to various machines, bags of liquid, and LED screens.

Officer Anderson pulled up a chair next to the bed and clasped her hands together. She appeared to shrink into herself, perhaps out of pity for me or respect somehow for the situation we found ourselves in.

When she spoke, it was in the same soft lilting voice that was incongruous with her uniform and firepower on her person.

"You were found unconscious in your yard by the Alston Fire Department, three-quarters dead." She smiled from one corner of her mouth. "Now you are only half-dead." Serious again, she continued. "Your house was a total loss. We also traced your route from the house that was going up on Ovist Road, which also burned completely down." She looked down into her hands again, and then looked up eyes fixed on mine. She had a fleck of blue in her green eyes.

"What happened with Davey and his partner?"

"They tried to kill me, and may have succeeded," I said. "After coffee, Davey shot me front and back with a nail gun, and then kicked me backwards into the basement. Then they covered the stair opening, poured gas over the entire floor deck, and set everything on fire." I paused. "Where are my dogs?"

She looked down again and half-wrung her hands out. "We found them lying together in the driveway. The black dog did not . . ." She paused, and a tear dropped out of the corner of one eye.

I turned away as tears filled my own eyes. I spoke from a place far away, outside of myself, a pit forming inside me at the loss of my beloved Satch. "And what about Grey?"

"If you mean the Shepherd, he was at the shelter."

"Was?"

She gave me a half-embarrassed glance, and in an inimitable gesture, brushed a lock of brown hair behind one ear. "I took him home after three days."

Three days? "How long have I been here?"

"Today is Saturday," she said. "You were brought in late on Wednesday afternoon."

Davey and Ferret Face must be long gone by now. "What about Davey?

She got up and walked to the window.

"Davey and Zack Morris were found dead in a Red Chevy pickup. Burned nearly beyond recognition."

"Where?"

"A thousand feet down the road from your driveway."

I was stunned, and I am sure my reaction would have been discernible on my normal face, but the wide-eyed, open-jawed manifestations were impossible in my current swollen state.

She looked down and over at me. "Davey's wife is filing murder charges."

"Against who?"

"You."

Chapter 16

"Different doctors and detectives from the Michigan State Police have been in and out of your room the past three days," Officer Anderson continued.

"Davey shot me with a nail gun and kicked me into the basement," I interjected. "Then started the house on fire."

She looked away again.

"Please look at me," I implored.

"I can't say any more."

"They think I shot myself? In the back? Then fell face-first 10 feet onto a concrete floor?"

"Constantine, I can't speak about this to you. You will have a chance to give your statement."

I averted my gaze to the ceiling. Strange plaster patterns were swirled into a reflection of my current mental maelstrom.

I heard a scuffling noise in the hallway, raised voices and cursing.

"I don't care if he is half-dead, I will finish the job!" Sobbing, then a scream. Despair laced with anger, the anguish clawed at the walls and tile floor, carrying into my room. I could hear, too, the officer stationed outside the room trying to reason with the woman.

I didn't need this. Two men tried to kill me, I barely survived, and now this. I tried to turn on my side, and pain lanced through me, front and back. I flailed with one good arm at unseen daggers.

Bella reached over, concerned, a look of dismay on her face. I also saw pity. Whether the pity was for my condition or for the sorry state of my future, I couldn't say. Most likely a bit of both.

"I need to go. Conn . . ." Her voice caught, she half-reached a hand to her mouth, and in a huskier tone said: "I am glad you are awake and healing."

She didn't say she was glad I was alive, and that was telling.

"Thank you for checking up and me and watching my dog. Can someone try to reach . . ." I struggled to finish and find the right words. "Lauren, my wife . . . ex, whatever?" I looked away, not knowing for sure what she was at this point in time.

"Your dog is heartsick and won't leave the front door. And yes, we are trying to reach her. Are there any other family members we should contact?"

I pondered that. Sadly, no.

"He likes toast," I said. "Grey. The crust. Make some and peel off the crust in pieces and he will warm up to you."

She smiled, maybe a bit wistfully, cocked her head a few degrees, and turned to go.

I watched her leave, and then heard the raised voices again as she and Davey's wife went at it. I was glad the door was closed. I almost wished it could lock, and I wished I could hit

84

the lights, draw blackout the curtains, and curl up and sink back into oblivion. But that could wait. I needed to prepare for war.

That night I dreamt of consuming fire and a gaping, beckoning abyss. The roar of approaching thunder and crimson flames terrified me, and I was again staggering away from disaster, a wall of licking flames looming overhead the slamming into me with devastating effect.

I recoiled from the stunning blow, awake now, to see a dark form with an upraised fist, ready to slam my midsection again. I thrust up a protecting arm and tried to twist away from the hammer.

The figure swung again, catching me on my side. Wildly, I grabbed at air, my good hand finding the IV stand, which I grasped and threw at the intruder. A grunt, and then in the half-light, I saw a flash of a face though the fog of awakened sleep. It staggered under the blow, and leapt on to the bed, gloved hands tearing at wires and tubes. The form kicked out with a knee as I fell off the other side of the bed, my hips and side finding the floor — hard, cold, and very painfully. I yelled at my attacker, scrambling on the slippery floor in my bare feet. I ripped out the remaining wires, reached again for the IV stand, and swung. It caught him high up, and he too fell with a thud to the floor. I heard the impact, unseen between the beds. I heard no sound beyond my heavy and ragged breathing, a wolf pup at bay, pawing at the night.

I moved around the end of my bed and found a pool of blood around the figure's head, atop the wheel frame of the adjacent bed. Out cold. I decided one more tap with the now-broken arm of the IV stand was warranted. In my abating rage, I stopped after three. If they awoke, a few broken ribs and a bruised torso to match their inflicted attack on me would be lingering caution to them.

It was a man, clean shaved, and closely cropped black hair. And he was wearing a uniform. Even more concerning was the lack of any response or alarms throughout the wing of the hospital. It was as if everyone disappeared. Or allowed the attack.

What had I gotten into?

Out of the corner of my eye, I saw a shard of silver. A spray of red swept across my eyes, and then blackness overtook me, an inky wet wilderness that dragged me in as I mentally drowned. I heard voices which echoed like calls of hyenas in my subconscious, laughing and gleefully inviting me to destruction.

Chapter 17

The bright light shining in my eyes and the hand on my forehead awakened me. The train racing toward me in my half-conscious dream state had stopped inches from my face. The back of my head felt as it some of my skull was missing, and little men with tiny sledgehammers were attacking what was left with a vengeance. I heard a far-off voice murmur that I seemed to be coming to. I also heard a woman's voice. Hoping it was my wife, that she had come back to see me, I tried to focus my eyes in its direction, only to find my new friend, Officer Anderson, there.

Disappointment must have shown in my face because the hard line of her mouth softened as she spoke.

"Not happy to see me, Constantine?"

I resisted a few sarcastic replies, and as I tried to speak, found the words difficult to force out of my throat. "Not to see you, it is just that you often appear after very painful circumstances arise." I tried to grind out the words over a sandpaper tongue. "Maybe next time it could be a general call, maybe with a cup of coffee?" I swallowed. "Did someone contact my wife?" I breathed deeply and continued. "Does this current state give me any leverage in proving my innocence for any murders?

"I couldn't say, other than that people are getting creative with attempts to kill you." She held up a one-gallon plastic Zip-Loc bag filled with what appeared to be IV tubing and data cables. "And yes, my people are trying to reach your wife."

She frowned at my questioning look. "We found these wrapped around your throat. We thought they had completed their task." She smiled, half-embarrassed. "At least they didn't use phone cord."

I rolled my eyes at her attempt at humor and tried to grin to remove any malice. It turned out to be a painful exercise. I clawed at my throat, catching my breath again. It felt like two or three anacondas had taken turns trying to strangle me to death.

"You saved your own life." Her hazel eyes turned again to the floor, and her voice caught, then faltered on. "You were able to get a couple fingers behind the cords, but as far as we can tell, you were out cold from the blow."

"What happened to the other guy?"

"What? The person who attacked you?" She gave me a quizzical look, again the suspicion rose in her face. She and the other officer with her shrugged at each other. "Conn, there was no one on the floor." Her look was half concern, half thinly veiled doubt.

"The guy that was in a pool of blood under the other bed there. I hit him with my IV pole."

Again, the shared look, much like mental health care workers sizing up a patient for a straitjacket.

"We found no bodies, there was no blood." Again, the shared look. "You must have dreamed that after being knocked out. "Your IV pole is right behind you."

I clawed at the neck of my gown, trying with difficulty to rip if down over my chest. There was a massive bruise in the center of my chest. "Care to explain this particular blunt force trauma?"

Bella paused, half-reaching toward my chest, then clenching her hands, pulled them back. "It looks like you ran into a tree."

"Sure, one growing sideways. How do you explain the cords around my neck?"

Again, the hesitation. "The doctor felt you tried to kill yourself."

Damn it. "Caved in the back of my skull, and then tried to strangle myself? Oh, sure, that makes sense." My finely tuned sarcasm bowstring was getting pretty taut and ready to snap. Was that the buzzing twangy noise I was hearing?

"Others are saying you tried to hang yourself with the cords and fell backwards trying to get out of bed."

"Okay, I get it; hang myself with a cord four feet off the ground. Nice detective work."

She looked hurt, like a dog just smacked on the head. A flash of resentment was present, mostly hurt.

I held up what was left of my good arm, palm out. "No, I am sorry, that was uncalled for. I am just getting tired of attempted murder. Mine. Next, a car will fly through the window to crush me."

"We are in the back of the hospital, Conn," a sharp twinkle in her eye. I liked her. Not everyone gets my groggy, half-dead, murder attempt survivor humor.

"A crane boom, then, or someone with a linen cart." I tried a weak smile, a thousand nerve endings all aligning in the folds of my cheeks and dimples. I closed my eyes, mentally clenching against the needles stabbing every square inch of my upper torso.

All my visitors ultimately left, and I was left trussed and wired and tubed up in my bed, with another guard posted down the hall. I resolved to leave that night.

Chapter 18

After midnight, I wheezed my way out of bed and pushed my IV rolling stand and monitor down the hall. My guard called after me, half-asleep himself in the lounge at the end of the hall. I hissed back that my toilet was plugged in my room, and I needed to use the one down the hall.

It better be plugged, I thought. I had shoved two hand towels down it.

I lurched my way around the corner and went into the janitor's closet next to the bathroom, where I unrolled a set of clothes I had hijacked from the closet in a man's room next to mine. I had sized him up with a brief glance through the door, and he appeared to be my size, perhaps a bit smaller.

Knowing cameras would be examined tomorrow, I made no effort to conceal my trip to the rear entry, which let me into the rear parking lot to the hospital, a washed-out faceless blacktop morass, fringed by the dark shadows of pine forest. A friendly deputy had responded to my earlier call and driven my truck over to the lot. Keys in the box. I struggled to get an arm over the box edge and stifled a scream when something tore open somewhere on my bruised and battered body.

I eased out of the parking lot, knowing I needed to retrieve something very important from my property. Then I had to find a hiding place to heal, and a place to plot my vengeance.

With my fuzzy mental state, perhaps 'plotting' was a bit much. But my inner animal nature was asserting itself, and was awakening a primal urge to strike out and fight back. A nameless force was trying to destroy me and my world. I would have something to say about that.

The drive home was deliberate and seemingly endless. When I arrived, I slid and staggered across my lawn in the darkness, making my way to the dark fringes of my yard along the creek, holding onto the thinnest strand of hope that my box had been flung far enough to be undetected. I panicked, on my knees in slick mud, feeling around.

There. Thank God.

I sat on the ground, all but hugging the metal-edged case: a life preserver of sorts. Quite literally. I could smell the burnt ash from my house, and vaguely see the skeletal framework of the nightmare that had been my home. I could smell the charred remains of my possessions and taste ash in the still air.

I staggered around the charred foundations of the house and tripped on some churned-up ground near the small garden shed by the ravine. I felt down and around, dropping to my knees. My hand found a small wooden cross with a dog collar hung around it. Someone had buried my precious boy. I wept and sensed the salt burning my cheek. I knelt there, amid the scent of burnt pine, as the night faded. I knew a search would be launched soon, but I needed time here. For him.

As a feeble illumination dawned on the eastern horizon, I patted the grave and rose, driving without headlights to the ball field where I had spent so many days on in my youth. The bleachers splintered and worn, red paint flaked off, slowly coming into resolution in the early morning light. My truck was parked behind the outfield wall, and I was huddled in the dugout, spreading out the contents of the box on the benches around me. I shivered in the early morning air, my only added protection being a flannel-lined work shirt I always left hanging in the shed. The quilted lining was smoky and familiar, a touchstone to a simpler time. It had been my grandfather's. He had met face-first many a frosted morning with uplifted eyes wearing this jacket of sorts.

I could smell coffee carrying in the thin air from an early riser. I wouldn't go undetected for long.

The box was more of a metal-rimmed suitcase with hard sides, and I had packed it as a go-box in case of an emergency. The word "emergency" seemed insignificant in light of my past four days. I reached first for the high-tech, breathable, heat-deflective shirt and pants. I struggled into the form-fitting fabric, feeling a modicum of warmth rising as I did. My arm gave me the most trouble; I had to wrestle the shirt sleeve over it. Most important, I pulled a pair of black work boots from the bottom of the box, waterproof and insulated. They might prove to tilt what slim odds I had to live a little more in my favor. I laced them on with some satisfaction, trying to ignore the stabs of pain throughout my body. Indeed my feet were still pretty bruised and blistered from my headlong run along the creek.

I looked around the dugout at two small and powerful flashlights, a knit cap, two plastic-wrapped burner cell phones with prepaid plans, a sheathed knife, small heat packs, energy bars, and a canvas bag unzipped to carry these and many more items. I reached into the foam lining of the box, and extracted what was now a very important item, a 9-mm Smith and Wesson handgun with two spare clips and four boxes of ammunition. I silently fitted the holster across my bruised chest, sliding the weapon into place. An envelope lay before me, with a $1,000 in bills splayed out, along with my passport and various gift cards I could redeem in lieu of credit cards that could be tracked. I pulled on a knit cap, with its own camouflage pattern somehow incongruous in the pale light of that morning. Gloves next, I pulled them on, or rather grimaced them on. My hands were battered and covered with cuts and abrasions. The Kevlar-like fabric should help me, if I lived long enough to figure out what was going on.

My wife had laughed when I had first broached the idea of a survival kit, so I had prepared this on my own had kept it locked with a small combination lock, buried under blankets in the basement. I know why I kept a kit like this — dark experience begat dark thoughts.

I felt a buzz, and a microsecond later, the air reverberated with a rifle shot. The air was soon filled with shots, swarming around the dugouts and bleachers. Someone was firing from a location just across the highway. I was tucked in the quiet shadows — they must have seen my truck and knew I was in the area. The echo of the explosions broke briefly, and I could hear the hiss of air from the truck tires. Moments later, sharp clangs carried across the field to me, like swords upon steel shields. They were firing down the sides of my truck. The gas tanks . . .

The explosion of light and sound tore apart the dawn as streaks of metal and flame arced around the ball field. I stuffed the remainder of the gear into the canvas bag and risked a quick glance around the corner of the dugout, where I saw the flash of the rifle from a truck parked across the road. Gripping my own gun, I eased out from the back side of the field, toward the west. I needed to flank the shooter (or shooters), since there was no way I was going to outrun them.

Limping across the highway, two houses down, I made my way through backyards. My truck, still burning mightily, was casting shadows over the position of my unseen enemy. I could see two men staring into the flames across the road, seemingly entranced by the glorious conflagration.

But it would prove to be their undoing. I came up behind them, and fired low, taking them both out at the knees.

They both collapsed within an arm's length of each other, their curses rising above the roar across the highway. I could make out their features. The Haakanen brothers. Always looking for trouble.

This time, they had found it.

I loosed two more rounds for good measure, one each in a knee. Rising from my half-crouch, which had been a painful exercise, I hobbled over and kicked away their rifles. One was a .306 with a scope — a hunting rifle. The other was an AR-15, a civilian version of a military M-16. They glared up, white eyes wide with fear and hatred, hurling creative invective at me.

"Why were you trying to kill me?" I had Jason, the oldest, by the front of the shirt, shaking him as if answers would tumble out like a jammed vending machine. I got two words in response.

I introduced the butt end of his AR to his nose, and from the immediate reaction, the short meeting drew satisfactory results. His head thudded off the ground, and I turned my attention to his brother, Jerry.

"Jerry, any interest in sharing the reasons why you tried to kill me?" I was well-aware that the police and fire departments were minutes away by this point.

Initially, there was no response. He continued his murmuring invective, with a few singular words repeating themselves.

We were eye to eye now, seeing the reflection of the sunrise and the inferno reflecting in each other's eyes. The mere seconds dragged in a seeming eternity to a full minute or more. I knew he saw the resolution in my eyes.

"He said to take care of you," he stammered at last. "The others missed you at the hospital. You were to be gone overnight."

He broke off, choking back the pain as he came out of shock.

He rocked back and forth, holding his drawn-up knees.

"Who?" I asked again, this time with more force.

More invective. I knew I had to go.

I threw the rifles in the back of their truck and remembered to check on his brother. He was breathing, eyes open and glaring at me.

I could only think of one place to go for any clue, and that was the old man's place out on Cemetery Road. I must have missed something before. I had just made the corner a half-mile away when I saw the lights of the response vehicles. In my rearview, I saw the headlights turning into the Fire Hall. I slowly made my way in the brothers' truck down the road, without headlights, and being careful not to gun the engine and throw up gravel on the narrow road. They would find me soon enough, and I didn't want to leave an obvious trail until I had a few hours to search the property.

This late in the fall, most of the leaves had fallen, and the forest cushion of golden poplar and red maple leaves glowed in the coming light. I curved past the small Laird Township cemetery on my right and continued down the dirt road. The sirens carried well in the cold morning air back here.

I was alive for now, and I missed my truck. This truck was a stinking beer-soaked garbage can posing as an ash tray, with little squares of tin foil scattered around the cab. There were numerous spiralbound notebooks. I grabbed one and scanned the first few pages, noting lists of names and addresses. A few caught my eye and surprised me. As I drove, more tiles started clicking into place.

Chapter 19

The small shack that had once been Simon's home had been burned to the ground. I shut off the truck, and slowly walked around the ashen outline. I kicked a few mounds over; light puffs of grey met my boots.

"He said you were a smart one!"

I whirled, gun in hand, the electric shock of the calm voice jolted me back here in the woods. It was a woman, grey in the uneven warmth of the rising sun, shapeless in heavy clothes.

"But he expected more from you," she continued. "Hell, I expected more."

I lowered the gun, eyes narrowing.

"Who are you?"

A pause, she looked around her into the surrounding field and forest.

"My name is Susan. I was a . . . friend of Simon's." No inflection. "My home is just down around the corner, why don't you come in, sit down and warm up?"

I opened the passenger door of the mobile ashtray, but she waved a hand and declined, turning and walking down the road away from me. I coasted behind her, all the while wondering when part of the search for me, either by law enforcement or growing cadre of enemies, would route them down this road. I knew that the road could get pretty rough ahead of me, but at least it was an outlet south, via the South Laird Road. I wasn't worried about how well the truck would take the road, as long as I got through it. I was wary, however, of Susan. I didn't know her, and I was sure I had not seen her before. She had a wiry, hard-bitten, independent aspect to her, and truthfully, I didn't trust anyone anymore. After a half-mile, she turned to her right, and headed towards the river. The doors of the truck, and at times, the hood, brushed back branches of maples and low-slung spruce trees. I wasn't getting out of here quickly.

The road, such as it was, curved down to the left into a small clearing by the creek. I could make out a snug little cabin with a moss-covered shingle roof, cedar siding, with small four-pane windows making a brave show on each wall.

She gestured for me to park, and then walked up to her small front porch before casting a speculative glance back at me. "You look like hell."

"Well, murder attempts tend to generally have that effect."

She laughed. "I never thought much of you, but maybe you'll do. Not everyone survives a murder attempt."

"Several, actually."

She raised an eyebrow.

"Well, I have been shot at with a variety of weapons, the first of which was improvised, I believe. Then let's see . . . strangulation, beatings, fire, gunfire, explosions. I sort of lost track after the first few dozen attempts. But it has only been a few days — we still have the rest of the week to reveal new and exciting ways to end me. I am thinking a bombing, strafing by a helicopter, chemical attack, and rabid squirrel bites, all would be pretty creative."

Now my humor was devolving into just flat-out pissed off. I wasn't sure I wanted to be in that cabin, but I needed answers. Gun in hand, I walked up the steps.

The cabin was cozy for a backwoods shack that I never knew existed. It looked very old, with rough-cut planking covering the walls along with old brass gas-lamps. The floorboards were of the same planking, with small worn areas beneath the small kitchen table and the living room in front of a stone fireplace. The ceiling was open and low, with exposed rafters of pine. It felt old, and had a scent of old parchment, wood smoke, tobacco, pepper, and vanilla. Most of the furniture appeared to be handmade, rustic pine with tucked calico fabric seats.

Susan gestured to a chair. She looked around the cabin, taking it what she knew was my initial assessment. "Old Henry did a pretty nice job on this cabin. It has held up well"

"Henry?"

"Oh, I think you know of whom I speak."

"Laird?" I asked. Her eyes sparkled as she took in my astonishment. "He homesteaded a mile west of here."

"Yes, but never built there, he built this back in the 1880s, before he and Archie started the whole 'we need our own township thing.'"

I was past being surprised I guess; my weariness and fatigue were catching up to me. "Archie McPhee, the guy who owned my property on North Laird Road?"

"One and the same. By the way, Archie never got over it being called Laird Road. Damn Henry got his name on everything, which was part of the deal." She squatted in front of the fireplace, using an old cast-iron poker to prod the embers of a fire into life. She added small pieces of cedar from a galvanized pail next to the stone hearth. She held out her hands, which flexed appreciatively as heat started to radiate out. She continued after a small cough as a wisp of smoke caught in her throat.

"How much did Simon tell you?"

"He told me an unbelievable story about Laird," I said. "And said it involved the Civil War. He left and said he would tell me the rest the following day." I paused. She knew what had happened next.

Susan looked at the floor; it appeared almost as if she was seeing it for the first time. Another slight cough . . . she balled her hands into fists and rotated them, stretching her forearm muscles.

"Simon told you about Henry Laird being a Pink," she said. "He spent most of the 1860s and 1870s tracking down Confederate war criminals and a treasure stolen by the Confederates. He assumed multiple identities, but most often just went under his own name, as the Laird name was well represented throughout the south. He tracked down stolen bonds, gold and silver bullion, Federal greenbacks and even

102

jewelry stolen by troops on both sides. During Reconstruction, fraud, as you know, was still rampant and there was still the specter of the Lost Cause."

She continued. "Henry Laird was sent to Upper Michigan in the 1870s to track former Confederate agents still working in the Great Lakes region. There was a thought there still could be what we would call terrorism today occurring immediately after the war. Reconstruction profiteering was rampant, trafficking in stolen goods still occurred on a large scale, and counterfeiting fell under the auspices of the nascent Secret Service as well, but the Pinkerton Agency had grown to a significant size and still handled contracting work for the Federal government. Henry also tracked several leads in the first 20 years after the war relating to treasure. I believe in your research you have heard several stories and theories regarding Confederate loot that's alluded to residing in the North."

I could still hear the keening of sirens a half-mile north, the creek acted as a natural sound conduit to carry even the rattle of yelling voices and the cacophonic sounds of various emergency vehicles arriving. One siren would abate, and another would take its place. I was enthralled by the story, but the needles of doubt and self-preservation kept striking chords in my body. I kept an eye on the door and a hand on my gun. I sat perched on the edge of a chair, anxiety drawing the bowstring of my spine taut.

My host showed no signs of tension or hurry and got up and walked over to the small kitchen. "Tea?"

She didn't wait for my response and continued, waving one hand in the air as if dismissing a vagrant breeze.

"While residing in Baraga, and working for the Duluth, South Shore, and Atlantic railways as an investigator, Laird became consumed with a pervasive rumor that Confederate treasure was buried somewhere in what is now Laird Township. He was especially interested in a small community forming known as Silver, which was founded by seven immigrants on homestead patents five miles down south from M-38. He struck up a friendship, and by design, became a leader in the nascent movement to form the new township. It was an inside joke in the family that Henry was actually advocating secession from Portage Township, which was and is, as you know, part of Houghton County. A Union spy promoting and advocating for township rights and rights of taxation. I think he took some private amusement in the irony of his advocacy. In 1887, the secession actually took place, as you well know, Laird Township was formed, with Henry Laird named as the first supervisor. As one of its first actions after that, a motion was carried to develop two roads in the township: one heading north two miles from the Baraga-Ontonagon stage road, one heading south five miles to the settlement of Silver."

"North Laird and South Laird Road," I interrupted.

"You got it." She paused and turned from the four-burner porcelain stove with her steaming kettle of hot water and poured it into delicate cups on the countertop. "You do know that Henry Laird didn't even homestead in the area until after

104

he had even been supervisor for two years?" She raised an eyebrow at me, a finely arched expression of amusement over her hidden knowledge. "He had this place to call home, the property owned by another Union veteran."

"That always bothered me," I said. "Along with the fact they let an outsider push his agenda and name the new township and roads after himself. Really strange."

She nodded knowingly and rubbed her two forefingers together. "A lot was at stake, but Henry was very persuasive, and also flashed around a lot of money and promises."

She again arched an eyebrow at me, and I was struck that, in her youth, she really must have been quite beautiful. She still maintained a measure of grace and fluidity of movement, and even with advancing age, her emerald eyes were indeed striking. A flash of youth still imbued her with a subtle elegance.

"You also presented the background of the Alston brothers, but you weren't able to make the connection with Henry Laird." She looked at me expectantly, knowing I could fill in some of my blanks.

"That's right," I said. "Joseph Alston had proposed a new railroad from Baraga south by southwest to Watersmeet, directly through Silver. The new railroad project was supposed to be headed by Alston himself, acting on behalf of six investors from Detroit."

She held up a hand, as if she were patiently waiting for the teacher to call on her. I smiled and nodded. She grinned. "Two of whom were former Confederate agents."

I actually recoiled from that information, struck dumb for a brief moment.

"Their intention was to move mining equipment into the Silver Mountain region and into the gorge to intensify the hunt for the treasure. But . . ." She continued." They didn't let Joseph know about the treasure. They just fed on his greed."

Chapter 20

"The railroad was supposed to be surveyed by Alston himself," I said, continuing the conversation with the old woman. "Through the Sturgeon Gorge Wilderness. The project cost a massive amount of money, and you can see the remnants of the grade started west from Baraga, down near the state park."

Susan nodded, and then motioned me to continue while she sipped her tea ss the sirens went silent along the creek. Someone would be coming this way soon — I knew it. Too many people were looking for me. But wanted to hear this story. Susan's eyes flashed impatiently, so I added: "Joseph and his brother David would ultimately plat and layout the village of Alston on the Mineral Range Railroad in 1899 and 1900."

She very nearly spat out her tea and pointed a thin finger at me. "On the site of the Village of Laird, named after Henry," she said. "That was done out of spite." She gazed into her cup, lost for a few moments on some private wave of thought. I took this as an impetus to continue the narrative.

"Joseph claimed he wanted the railroad to haul white clay from the Silver River to Baraga for use in a porcelain factory he was building, and also to open up millions of board feet of White Pine timber for use."

"What did you think of that information?" she interjected. "Do you feel that was the true reason?" She was regarding me over the rim of her cup.

"It feels like a cover story. All it would take is one hiking trip to the Sturgeon Gorge to see it would be incredibly expensive and foolhardy to run a railroad through that area. I felt Joseph had a scam going on. There is also very little white clay to be had along the Silver River." I had found notes by Orrin Robbinson, an early settler in the area, that the clay was tested and proved to be far too coarse for porcelain. An awful lot of money was expended, stolen, or lost during the venture."

"Damn right, it was a scam," Susan said. "Joseph was always on the lookout for easy money. He was jealous of his brother David, who later bankrolled the new venture in Alston, for David inherited a sizable amount of money from his wife's family estate. He also felt he had a right to whatever Henry found in the wilderness and tried to partner up with Laird in his search. He had sniffed around the saloons in Baraga for years and felt strongly that whatever spoor Henry had picked up on, he had a right to as well. Henry grew annoyed by Joseph's boldness and prying, and pulled in a few favors in Washington, D.C. to get Joseph's railroad stalled in court over property right of ways."

"Is that why Joseph went into the land business? He must have dragged David into it with even more talk."

"Yes." She coughed again, more violently this time, the echo resonating deep in her chest. "But all Henry wanted was a township he had the right to roam in and where he had the freedom to search for signs of the treasure."

She smiled enigmatically now. "Do you think there is treasure?"

"I believe there is something to draw so many people out to look for it." I stood and scanned the bank of the creek outside. "I also think there is some secret I must be close to that's making people want to kill me. Maybe to protect the secret?"

She tapped her forefingers on her cup, then set it down with a whispering ring on the small coffee table separating us. She rose and went over to a small bookshelf mounting at chin height on the east wall. She extracted a thin leathery volume from among the dozen or so perched there. She sat again, pulling on a string-clasp and opened the book in her lap. It appeared to be a ledger of sorts, or an oversized diary. The book was obviously very old, and I could hear the faint rustle of the parchment-like paper and the scent of decades that wafted up as she opened it.

She put on a pair of reading glasses from a string around her neck, winding the earpieces around each ear and scanning the pages with a forefinger. She let out a short exclamation and handed the book over to me. With some difficulty, I processed the flowing handwriting script. It was done with a fountain pen and India ink, and gradually I recognized words, and a different era came into focus with a modicum of clarity.

Sunlight was filtering into the room now, catching dust and imperceptible puffs of movement in its grasp. It was probably getting to be around 7:00 in the morning. I could almost feel an army of searchers mobilizing. My forearms felt itchy, and I rubbed one as I read with my good hand. The smell of the tea was filling the room as it warmed to the sun: lemon and honey. I was also hungry, but unfolding revelations overrode these needs. I could feel myself getting sleepy — the stress, lack of sleep, and injuries all melding in the warmth of the room, where the fire and sunlight had raised the temperature considerably. The smell of leather, old cloth, bleach, and wood smoke all blended comfortably in the small atmosphere of the cabin.

One often heard of the infinite seconds between the effects of a gunshot and the actual retort, and evidence of this unfolded in the slowest of motions in front of me. My host, looking expectantly at me while I read, gaped her mouth as a crimson bloom opened on her forehead, a look of shock and dismay as her moment of revelation came to reality and was taken away from her. I dove as the echo came, a concussive force of air and glass that erupted in the wall opposite me. The staccato impact of dozens of slugs into the walls of the cabin shook the foundations as I dove to the floor. I scrambled to reach my bag while my bad arm made its attempt to grasp my dropped pistol. It had been in my lap as I scanned the book.

The book. I crabbed across the room, trying to stay below windowsill-level, and grabbed a broom by the front door. Making my way back to the bookshelf high above me, I knocked the remaining volumes off the shelf and onto the floor. I stuffed them all in my bag, checked Susan's body for any signs of life and finding none, half-crouched, half-dove out the picture window facing the creek. I hit, impacting with a grunt and sharp intake of breath as the pain of opened wounds nearly overtook me, and then rolled down the grassy slope to the creek. Thickets of tag alder engulfed the banks both upstream to the north and downstream.

I glanced back and heard more gunshots and the tires exploding on the truck. I saw a figure rounding the east corner of the house, rifle to shoulder, sweeping the area. I fired shots toward him and saw him go down on one knee and aim his rifle toward me. Shots sprayed the woods around my position, so I crouched low and plunged to my left, south down the creek bed. Shots continued to clip the trees around me; the whine and echoes shattered the air like glass.

Mist was rising from the water around me as I half-ran downstream, trying to avoid any small pools that would be my end. At a bend in the creek, I dragged myself up a small chest-high bank. I was having difficulty drawing a breath. My lungs burned as if I was gulping acid, not air. I couldn't outrun anyone in my condition, so I made my way along the bottomland to a position back upstream facing my attacker, keeping low and hopefully out of his sightlines, assuming he was still on the creek.

Sunlight dappled the mist and I caught brief flashes of water as I moved as silently as I could. I brought my pistol to bear on a flash of movement, dropped my bag, and rushed to the water's edge. He saw me as I crested the bank and snapped off a shot, an angry hornet that clipped the top of my left shoulder. I leapt off the bank, hammering a shot down at him. I caught him high up, lost my pistol, and we both feel awkwardly. Falling back against the sand, he struggled to regain his feet, my hands reached for his neck, and I realized that it was Davey's brother, Josh. I half-rose and pounded my right fist into his exposed neck and face. He tried to get his arms in front of him to push me off, but I outweighed him and had leverage for the moment. The next few seconds became a crimson eternity, and I lost myself in my anger.

Josh lay unconscious in the sand. His ragged breathing told me he was alive, however tenuous that might be. We had not spoken or shouted one single word, threat, or warning. I was done in. I dragged him one-handed to a small shelf of rocks and arranged his body in a half-upright position before splashing back across the creek and finding my pistol in the sand. I made my way back to the place I dropped my bag. This bag not only held elements of my survival for the time being, but the books I had shoved in there before diving out of the window that may well hold the key to why so many people were trying to kill me.

Right now, all I could think of was to get Josh to wake up. In my rage, I had struck him pretty hard. I trussed him up with a small length of paracord and sat on a small ledge of rock 20 feet away. I could hear no other sounds of pursuers, nor any sirens. I did not know what happened to Josh's partner, who I had seen go down. The decision nagged at me whether or not to go back to the cabin. I needed food, but I also needed answers. I needed both quickly. Surely, I could not keep everyone at bay and elude capture much longer, and I did not trust law enforcement.

My shoulder stung where the rifle shot had come dangerously close, and I gingerly felt beneath my collar to a small groove that burned to my touch. I dipped into my bag, coming out with a small first-aid kit, fumbling with the waterproof seal before finding the tube of antiseptic gel. A few rough moments later, I got some of the contents into the general area. I could feel the numerous cuts and abrasions all over my body crying for some of the same treatment, and I knew some of the stitches had opened up. But I was alive. At least for a moment.

I opened the small leather-bound book and tried to ignore again my battered and bruised fingers. A couple of fingernails were black, and the backs of both hands were swollen. The leather-bound volume appeared to be a ledger or journal, filled with meticulous script, but with evidence of multiple hands writing in it. It was filled front to back. I turned to the last page that contained script:

November 7, 1907

Chapter 21

Morgan watched the wagons move out before dawn with wistfulness. He was about to lead a chase to divert attention away from those buckboards. His men would soon leave their camp in Indiana. The Federal cavalry would be moving fast but would be sure to pick up on the heavy wagons his men had commandeered and loaded with goods from the town. Morgan half-lifted a hand after the departing small caravan, knowing the drivers faced a perilous road ahead. He was confident in leading his men safely across the state, to recross the mighty Ohio River again as soon as possible, but the rising water and weeks of rain did start to worry him. But he knew their course was set, and as their wagons had a chance to change the tide of the war, he was willing to endure a great risk and harm to himself to accomplish this.

The wagons had to be taken apart before they loaded the Alice Dean in Brandenburg, and their cargo was laboriously transferred aboard. The heavy crates were labeled as munitions and took two men apiece to transfer, 24 in all. Any lingering questions by the men as to the contents of the boxes were silenced as cannons boomed from across the Ohio River in Indiana. A small contingent of Union troops had put up a brave front in trying to prevent the crossing. Morgan's men hastened their endeavors and got their four cannons broken down and loaded after dispersing the troops with a few well-placed shots of their own. A Federal 'tin-clad' gunboat also made a demonstration mid-river, much to the chagrin of the assembled Confederate force waiting to cross.

Basil Duke walked his horse over to his brother-in-law and commented between the booms of cannon: "I didn't know our good friend Mr. Hines was meeting us here." He was referring to Thomas Hines, the head of Morgan's scouts and a man of great sardonic wit and resourcefulness who was lounging on the south bank of the Ohio waiting for them to cross in Brandenburg.

"He ran a little errand, preceding us into Indiana."

"Sounds like things got a little hot for him." Basil was understating the situation, having come back with only a few of the 42 men he had started the raid with. "We still riding into that particular hornet's nest, Morg?" He was still a bit concerned his friend and brother-in-law hadn't shared that vital piece of information concerning a reconnaissance mission.

Morgan was looking across the Ohio, a faraway look in his eyes. His voice was softer as he spoke.

"We have to."

He walked away, and Basil swore he heard a few more words carrying back to him. "Too much depends on it." He too noticed that the general was carrying a lot of figurative weight on his shoulders. He still moved with confidence, but the easy and ready smile he had at the beginning of most raids was abeyant.

Chapter 22

The hush was almost reverential; the steepled bare maple branches overhead parted the morning and created a cathedral of light and vague form. The forest floor still glowed, and the crude altar of sand upon which my captive lay was highlighted by a gap in the canopy above. "Sacrificial" was the word that came to mind most readily. He had partially awakened and was shaking his head, trying to clear the fog and disorientation. He was very uncomfortable, but he was a killer, and yet one more person who had tried to take my life.

It was still difficult to ponder the fact I was being hunted all because of this secret I didn't know about, although my opponents thought I did

I was beyond fatigued, with my leaden consciousness threatening to bring its weight to bear and drag me into an abyss. Around me, I could feel the world spinning. Red and gold swirled and roared. I shook my heavy head and felt an ox-like ponderousness amid my surroundings. I was determined to somehow find the reason for my pursuit. I splashed water on my face, cupping small portions one-palmed.

I walked over to my captive and prodded him gently with a foot. Maybe it wasn't so gentle — he thrashed and fought against his gag and bindings. With one finger, I pulled the gag out and down.

"Why are you trying to kill me?" I asked.

His response was a cacophony of invective, spitting out vitriol.

I replaced the gag and prodded him again. He may have recoiled enough from my gentle persuasion to roll a few feet back into a pool of water. Panic shone in his eyes as he struggled, half in the water. I had no stomach for this, but I need answers. His muffled screams and swearing were scorching the creek bed black, but after a few minutes, turned to sobs.

I pulled the gag down again and he sputtered and moaned.

The roundhouse kick he tried toward my knees was painful. I returned the favor, and he just happened to once again roll into the water, face first. I had to move this along, others would be searching for me soon. I could hear distant shouts and vehicles racing down gravel roads south of the creek.

I hauled him half upright, bending his head back to expose his neck. It was painful to me, and I could feel the tiny demon cuts tearing again. I held on with my good arm, and had my hunting knife reverse-palmed, inches from that exposed white flesh. I drew it along the taut jugular, drawing the tiniest amount of blood. I finally saw the fatal fear, all bravado gone, and the last vestige of resistance faded over the horizon of his fate.

Throwing him down into the rocky sand, he grunted and gasped. His words were ragged and nearly inaudible.

"You came too close," he stammered. "Too many secrets."

The words came out chokingly, as a black chimney blows out soot, coughing as the fire of life sputtered there on the sand. Achingly, as his words drew upon a bowstring tuned to lies, misdirection and a finite knowledge; his story poured forth. His diction at once discordant music, shot through with chords of truth. "There is a treasure here in Laird Township from the Civil War. We believed that you were the one to finally find it."

I fixed him with my eyes, not wanting to speak. My own story-fabric was woven with broken thread and frayed connections, and I needed to take in this view that had one eye on my death.

"Then why try to kill me? Why not wait until I found the treasure? Why not wait until I had done your work for you?"

"Because we suspected she had the missing pieces."

"Who?" I asked. "Susan?"

A nod.

"Then why kill her?"

He stared at me. "The shot was meant for you."

Chapter 23

A chorus of caws and a hammering of wings saw a large number of crows take to the sky from the underbrush on the north creek bank. Something had scared them from their kill.

I remembered that a group of crows was called a "murder." Damned appropriate in my case. Something had startled them; I could hear the whine of engines, sounding like four-wheeler ATVs approaching our area. The off-road vehicle trail was nearby, they were probably searching for their guy and me.

Two crows were perched over my head, seemingly conversing with each other. They sat away from another group that confined itself to two trees overlooking their area of concern. My pair was nodding at one another, as if deriding the situation, saying "look at all those fools." Indeed. What secret could be worth all this killing? Money, power, influence, treasure? What 150-year old secret was that valuable?

The crack tore the quiet morning asunder. A soft grunt and I half-spun to see my captive's body stiffen and tumble over. Shots ranged around me. I kept close to the shallow bank, where the four-foot escarpment was shiny with red clay, overhung with grass and soil.

Voices echoed in the woods surrounding me, the high-pitched whine of small ATVs whirled in a discordant song. I could hear the distinctive thrum of at least five or six, split on both sides of the creek. They were closing in, and my unseen sniper was steadily dropping shots in the air around me. You would think he would stop given the crowd closing in.

I struck out downstream. A concussive force shook leaves from trees and boomed throughout the bottomlands. They had blown up the cottage, and I could see flames and plumes of smoke over my shoulder. I pressed on ahead.

I was climbing over a deadfall in the creek when I heard the bark of dogs. I wasn't sure how much direr the situation could get, but the point appeared to be fast approaching. I looked down at my hands, nearly blood-red with the clay, as if I did indeed had blood on my hands.

I had no choice but to press ahead. A shootout in the low ground would only get me killed. I knew the trail twisted away from the creek, so they would have to follow me on foot.

My Aunt Eunice lived a mile downstream, on South Laird Road, just up the hill from a bend in the creek. If I could get there, I could maybe get a change of clothes, some rest, and a vehicle. I also knew it was time to call in my reinforcements, or at least law enforcement. The images from the hospital were still fresh, and I mentally recoiled from the thought of a 911 call.

I ran and recreated my previous painful stumbling —half-blind, knee-slamming flight — downstream. I heard the hive-hum of the ATVs, now distant, sure they would head to South

Laird Road to cut me off. My sniper had fired a few rounds into my direction, and the shots had since stopped. He would probably have the same idea. I had to cut up a ravine and head north, hoping the dogs would take a while to follow my scent, with most of my shambling and limping steps in water. The rougher the country, the harder the pursuit . . . or so I hoped. I didn't have much left in me, but reserves were summoned. Impending death is a powerful motivator. Branches, rocks, grass, leaves, brambles were all a blur: slamming, scraping, and raking all parts of me. All nature turned a blind eye to any physical pain I was enduring.

***

"Conn, come in." Eunice looked around anxiously in her back yard.

I had near-crawled to her back door, shielded from the road by a small garage. She placed a hand on my shoulder as I nearly fell through the doorway. Concern flooded her face, or at least what passed for an attempt at concern.

Eunice was my uncle's youngest sister. She had lived near Detroit for many years, working for an accounting firm.

When her husband died 15 years ago, she had retired and moved back to the area. She was petite, whip-lean, and weathered. For a hobby, she boarded horses and raised them on a small farm. I could hear them whinnying in the back corral, just around the garage and near a large pole-building that served as a barn.

She was near 60, her hair grey and worn short. She had always taken a somewhat of a kind interest in me, and had me over for a few meals over the years. Lines creased her face, deep enough to arouse interest in her story, each a whisper of a concern or tragedy in her past. Her eyes were flinty and flashes of a golden past sometimes shone through.

"You need a shower, food, and sleep," she told me.

"I need a phone first." I reached for the phone on the wall next to the refrigerator.

"I am afraid I cannot let you do that, Conn." Weary with lack of sleep and a punishing journey, I turned and peered out from under heavy eyelids to see her standing with a pistol. A drawer was open next to her.

"You have got to be kidding, Eunice." I really was getting weary of betrayal and being shocked into silence. "So you would sell out your family to save your house?"

She looked down, shame and lack of resolution radiated out from her being.

"That isn't all, my boy." A male had appeared behind her, coming into the kitchen from the living room. Yancy Carmichael, Eunice's on-again, off-again boyfriend. He had his sallow, sunken face and yellowed teeth, decaying from cigarettes and probably meth. His stare was lupine and fixed, eyes strangely dilated in the light of the kitchen and from his moment of perceived triumph.

He reached for a handset on his belt. "We have him. South Laird Road." Short, staccato static bursts followed as my searchers buzzed in acknowledgment.

"I am not your boy, Yancy."

"I think you are. You always had a smart mouth. Enjoy the last 10 minutes of your life. Why don't you have a seat, the guys will all be here soon."

To say my mind raced would be an understatement, but the threat sharpened what was left of my reserves, already stretched out on a rack of the last few days. My gaze fixed on Eunice, who stood, abashed, pistol hanging by her side. Death was most likely closing in on her as well. Even if she did survive the day, this would haunt her. Even now her facial features were waxen and drained white. I was reminded of a candle nearly burned out, the wick melted into molten remains of a once happy life.

Chapter 24

My life was swirling in that moment, slowing down in the most painful replay. Colors and images flashed as the world arrested itself in this frozen fragment of time. The faces of those with me cast themselves in a frame from which I could ascertain doubt, fear, insecurity, hatred, envy, and above all, truth.

In this fragment, I leapt forward, slamming my aunt's hand against the wall above their old rotary telephone. I grabbed the handgun and reversed it to cover the old she-wolf and her mate. Under cover of the gun and the yellow light of a warming afternoon, I stumbled into the bitter ash of a shattered moment in my personal history: full of questions about family, fate, and now, fortune.

I dragged both of their trussed-up bodies into the living room, smashed the phones, and gagged them both. With a gun in his mouth, there was a lot less bravado and yapping emanating from that particular individual.

Before the gag went in, my aunt whispered in her rasp: "Carlyle." I had no clue what she meant.

I slashed the tires of her old Subaru, and jammed Yancy's Chevy pickup into gear, an old 1990-ish faded blue beast. I pulled out of the driveway, with a sudden, dawning realization of where I could possibly find answers. It was just over a mile away, and what I needed was to get there and escape detection in this vehicle. No one knew that I had it, and my pursuers had not shown up yet, but I could hear their engines whine.

I turned cautiously onto M-38, then immediately crossed the road and turned onto Alston Avenue. After a short distance uphill, with the asthmatic old truck wheezing at the grade, I turned into the lot of the Laird Township town hall. Driving around back, I put the transmission into low gear, parking in the lot behind the salt barn of the adjacent county road commission. Out of sight, I cautiously kept low across the parking lot.

From my presentations, I had been given a key to the town hall, and with it, I let myself in. Careful to turn on no lights, I made my way to the records room and sat at an old table.

From my knapsack, I gently removed the blood-gained old diary, and spread out the remnants of my meager possessions, the handgun placed on the table next to me. I prayed I would not have a shootout in the confines of this musty and historic place in both my and the township's history.

I trembled from the accumulated stress and nearly collapsed into the chair, my breathing heavy and ragged with apprehension and my own fear. Whatever I might find, it would be in the township records, this diary, and in the clue "Carlyle."

A wilderness of mirrors blocked my mental vision and misdirected me. I could hear the drums of truth pounding in the jungle of my thoughts. Red eyes stared at me from the recesses of darkness, where half-formed questions and elusive answers swirled in my consciousness.

I thought back to my aunt twisting in upon herself, contorting the person I knew her as into a half-crazed beast, snapping against the unseen chains of bad decisions. Manacles of compromise had left her mental ankles and wrists bloody with struggle. When she looked up, wounded by conscience, and rasped out the one word, it had been one last act of contrition she could offer.

Chapter 25

I had to focus, listening for the thrum of my pursuers: whines of sirens, squeals of vehicles, shots, and shouts engulfed the neighborhood.

I made a few calls from the landline and then sat down to work. I first reached into my battered bag, lifted out the worn leather volume, and turned through the pages, creamy brown and brittle, nearly parchment to the touch. A few entries dated in the 1860s appeared a few pages in, and then the handwriting changed, finally transforming into a beautiful script near the end. It appeared less of a diary and more so the personal notes by three individuals. It took my eyes a brief moment to adjust to a scratchy cursive from 150 years ago. A peculiar heavy slant to the flowing letters made some deciphering laborious, but left me astonished nonetheless:

I, Thomas McGhee, lay pencil to this paper as a record of what I have done, seen, and heard. I, being ardent to the cause, lay forth this story of personal courage and a mission yet unfulfilled. It is my intent, that should I fall in service by the hand of those opposed to me, this record may yet remain to serve as inspiration for those who would take up the flag of freedom from oppression and Northern aggression.

General Morgan detailed Peter Heinzman, George Finerly, Isaac Strong, and myself to deliver two wagons north from southern Indiana during his Great Raid in July of 1863. He demonstrated against Union militia on the bluffs at Vernon before withdrawing his men southeast. We were instructed to hide the wagons in a barn until afternoon, change into Yankee uniforms, and head north, swinging wide to the west around Vernon. When questioned or stopped, we said we were hauling coal for the prisoner of war camp at Camp Morton in Indianapolis. When past that point, we were to indicate we were heading to Camp Douglas. In reality, we were headed with our delivery to Michigan, specifically the far north. We were questioned by a few patrols, but the vast majority of Yankees we encountered were headed south or setting up defenses in case our men made a run north.

Peter and I were both sergeants, but Peter was a sour old man of 30 who had his own ideas about running the operation. I insisted that orders were given to me, and I am sure many could hear our whispered arguments at times. George and Isaac were both 18, excited and nervous, but kept out of our arguments. Peter demanded we uncover the wagons and find out what we were hauling. One night, he finally pulled back a tarp to reveal, indeed, a full wagon of coal. He climbed in and started throwing around coal, expecting to find treasure I guess. He gave up, sooty and black in the fading light. A drawn pistol on my part encouraged him to re-tarp the wagons and climb back on.

We were on a Yankee mining and stagecoach road north of Green Bay, still heading north. George and Isaac were nervous, with the prospect of patrols and a Union prison stay looming large in their minds. We had changed out of the military uniforms, leaving them weighted down by rocks in a stream miles back.

We were dressed in rough, homespun teamster's clothes, and were not harassed until we reached the Michigan border. We were passing through a logging town, trying to make time. We had been riding north with our cargo for two weeks. Isaac bought a newspaper from a boy into the second week and the news was centered on the war effort and especially the alarm raised by our boys, now scampering across Ohio, heading home. We needed a few more days. I had promised Captain Hines we would be at our destination within three weeks.

General Morgan raised hell throughout the raid, and generally made a nuisance of himself. It felt good for all of us to bring the war north. We sorely felt the effects of war in Kentucky. I desperately missed the fine hills of my home on the perilous journey.

We did encounter a precarious grade down to a river bottom once we got into Michigan a ways. A local man had asked if we were headed to the mines, I assured him we were. George sniggered at me whenever I tried a Yankee accent on for size, but it got us along.

At the river bottom, waiting for passage on a narrow bridge over a clay-filled muddy river, we had words and an altercation with a group of horsemen claiming to be a local *police force. They were led by a white-bearded man named Wesley or Welsey. Shooting was involved, and in a desperate charge over the river, Peter lost his wagon over the railing and was swept away in the muddy waters. George had dismounted from the wagon with a rifle and was steadily emptying saddles. Our attackers numbered eight; they were down to four with two of them wounded as we made our way across the bridge. Isaac had a burn from a gunshot and was shaking when he hopped up on the wagon. George had leapt onto the load and was calmly spraying shots back along the riverbank.*

Knowing pursuit would soon be coming if they dared tell the real authorities, we left the main military road, which was in fact a quagmire of slippery clay, and headed east on a logging road. I soon found that both Isaac and George were bleeding something fierce from gunshot wounds.

We found a logging camp, and a man passing as a camp doctor puttered and attended to their wounds as best he could. The rough men had a lot of questions, but when I described our attackers, they knew their leader well. They were a hardened lot of bushwhackers and thieves, making money kidnapping women and girls for trade of a repugnant sort: servicing miners and loggers. With so many good men off to the war, these blackhearts roamed the backwoods and rivers of Michigan pretty much with impunity. I felt the questioning looks and inquiring glances of many of our hosts, and felt that they may not be much more morally advanced than those we met at the river.

Leaving Isaac and George to the doctor's not-so-tender mercies, I left with the wagon, indicating that I was headed for help and a real doctor. I felt badly for them, suspecting the worst of the lot, but I had no choice. My mission and cargo were vital.

I pulled off into deeper woods at night and travelled for one whole day plus another night. The going was very slow on the rutted and rough woods road. I became aware of pursuing horsemen, whether the bushwhackers or loggers from my camp, I could not say. Shots rang out the second evening, and one hit me in my left shoulder. A looming mass rose up along my left, and I coaxed the horses towards the large shadow in the day's fading light. I made out a dark hole in the face of a large embankment, and drove the wagon in. There was barely enough room to unharness the horses, but I did, and got them around the wagon. I led them outside, scanning for my pursuers, and led them a mile south to another swiftly flowing river. I tethered them there and returned up to the cave. I removed two sticks of dynamite and blew the entrance. The results were quite satisfactory to me. I blew off two more at the river to draw my pursuers away from the cave and continued northeast from my position with one of the horses leading the other, who had a set of saddlebags on her. She also had a bullet furrow on her left flank and was losing a lot of blood. I stopped at a creek after midnight, with the moon obscured behind clouds. I slept but minutes, with my rifle hard by me, knowing my pursuers would be soon behind me.

As the sky lightened, I heard the snort of horses through the trees, and lay in the dense undergrowth along the creek. The voices of three men called out in the morning silence. I was being hunted. But just like the General, they were diverted away from the real source of interest. My saddlebags were worth the hunt, however. I needed to take care of them.

I played a game of cat and mouse and dropped a few more sticks of dynamite along my trail. I dropped one in a beaver hole on a side stream, another in a cave near a larger river. The explosions put my pursuers back on my path. I had one last stick that I used to great effect on a chalky bluff along the south side of a promontory. I had found a small hole in the yellowish-white face and lit the fuse. This last charge was surely the most spectacular, with dust settling in the evening sunset. Great was the glorious light of the western sky, all reds and yellows, laced with the bitterness of a possibly failed mission.

One horse, the grey, collapsed near a large pine, which was the largest I had ever seen. The wounded roan made another few miles before she collapsed. Regretfully, I helped them each into oblivion, ashamed that wolves would soon erase their mortal remains. I had slung the saddlebags about me and fell many times in delirium and weakness from my wounds. Unsure of my pursuers' location, I kept waiting for the shot that would end me. Somewhere, I don't remember exactly where, I buried the bags into the base of a lightning-marked maple, along a sweeping bend of another river as it curled back upon itself. I would come back, as I would for the wagon.

Chapter 26

My eyes were getting sore. The story was enthralling, but the script was difficult to decipher and was getting more erratic. I was soon to find out why that was.

I went to the windows of the town hall and noticed no untoward activity at the road or the neighboring houses. I was undetected as of yet, but it wouldn't last long

My eyes and body nearly betrayed me, such was my fatigue. Heavy lead weights pulled my eyelids down, wrestling with my burning hate for unseen forces pursuing me, along with a trace of fear.

My narrator continued:

I ended up after a terrible flight at a mission on Lake Superior, where my wounds are being treated by a kindly Indian woman and a man of the cloth. I didn't catch much of their speaking, which was in a language unknown to me. Of course, all languages but English are unknown to me, anyway.

I ended up fighting a fever, and was kept for nearly a month, in and out of delirium. I was given this journal to keep time and compose my thoughts. The Indian woman was uncommonly beautiful and returned my stolen glances I furtively cast from my sick bed. I still remember those dark

eyes and half-smile. The priest called her Susan. A kindly French trapper took me by canoe to a lively pair of towns straddling a wide inlet off the Great Lake. In broken English, he explained that to go further required a portage on the north end. He waved off my offered coin, saying I "would need it."

There were a few blank pages in the journal, and then a few had random words and strange drawings that looked like small hieroglyphics. The lines dragged off the pages and appeared to be something a child would render. Then a chill overtook me in that chair . . . I turned the page to find one last entry:

I am dying, not much left. The fever has never left. I have paid a king's ransom for my board, and now they must bear the burden of my mortal husk. I leave this record hoping someone will complete my mission. I know not what happened to George and Isaac; I thought someday they would look for me. I do not regret my service. Tell the General I tried . . .

The words tailed off.

I ran my palms over the face of my eyes and finished the motion by running them over my temples and to the back of my head, where I let one weary hand linger and rub away at my sore neck. Hell, I was sore all over. A sharp rapping on the rear door awoke me. I was in a quiet office, so I just waited. One more time, then whoever it was stopped.

Carlyle.

A small alarm was ringing in my head, but my head was pounding, so it felt more like drums. I made my way to the township records room. I had spent a lot of research time in there, so I pulled up some old township tax ledgers. I started looking through names — Archibald, Heikkinen, Drew . . .

Nothing. I ran through a few more years — 1905, 1906, through the 1920s . . . I scanned a few pictures on the wall, historic photos and froze on one. It showed the town hall, next to an old Methodist Church and what was now the Alston Apostolic Lutheran Church, which was at that time an old school.

Carlyle.

There were a few file folders on local businesses kept in the top drawer of a yellowed file cabinet. I scanned a few, keeping an ear out for any potential visitors returning to the door.

I found an old reference to a property transfer deed. The Methodist church got dismantled and moved to 20 miles east to L'Anse in the 1930s. I searched through a few names. There. Joshua Carlyle, Pastor. The alarm bells in my mind were jangling.

Now what exactly could that name or person tie into? I couldn't guess at the moment, but it was a clue. I knew from past research that the church had moved to the hill overlooking the football field in L'Anse, just up from Broad Street. I remembered seeing it there in the 1970s, before that too burned down.

I sat and picked up the narrative again. A few pages in, another hand appeared. Again, it took a while to follow the flow of the old-fashioned cursive script, an almost feminine hand this time. I read on:

July, 1884

I take pen in hand to honor the substance of this journal, given to me by my father, who tried for many years to solve the mystery related in these previous pages, retrace the steps taken by this Confederate gentleman, and ascertain the wagon location and the cargo detailed therein. He wasted years wandering all over the wilderness, walking streams and rivers, travelling here in both Michigan and Wisconsin, months on foot and horseback. Never found a clue other than a frayed bit of harness amidst some bleached horse bones along the river. It took his health and wasted the dreams of our family. I have nothing but the coin that he gave to me as a talisman, when he told me to never stop dreaming or searching. I have not stopped dreaming, but I have stopped searching. Perhaps my children will one day set forth and find things I cannot.

I heard a key turning in the lock at the rear door of the town hall. I gathered my journal and a few of the files and stepped into the bathroom. I heard a person enter, and also their footfalls as they made their way across the hardwood. Another door opened, and then a slight creaking. A file drawer was slid open. I waited silently, though I was sure they could hear my pounding heart. A light glow filtered around the corner from the office as a light was turned on. Then I heard the sounds of someone exiting and the door slammed shut. But I still sensed . . . something.

I padded out quietly, paused at the doorway, saw a flash of movement, and ducked. I felt a whiff of air.

Chapter 27

I first took in the middle-aged woman and then the snow shovel that had been used to nearly level me. She had it raised up like a sword.

"I heard you in the bathroom, and pretended to leave," she said. "I don't know what you were doing in here, Mr. Constantine, but you should not have been screwing around in the archives."

"Marge, why did you try and take me out? Put down the damn shovel!"

She frowned and looked down begrudgingly at the weapon, then propped it against the wall. I was half-leaning against the old wood-pattern 1970s paneling and seemed to be standing in a small pile of dead flies. Marge was the township treasurer, a matronly widow in her late 50s; I knew she had the position for a great number of years.

"Why were you skulking about, Conn?"

"Honestly, Marge—"

"Conn, as soon as someone says the word 'honestly,' I am already doubtful."

"Some people are after me." She frowned and raised one skeptical eyebrow at me, a slight tilt to her head. The intonation of her posture invited me to continue.

"Evidently, some bad people are convinced I know something."

Lines furrowed at her temples, and she reflexively clenched one hand.

"I just need some time to dig through some files, and then I could use a ride out of here."

Her look spoke of many questions but did not hesitate. "I will be at my computer. Whistle when you are ready. I have to make a few entries."

A few pickups rumbled by outside, moving quickly north. Another flashed by 20 minutes later, heading south. Evidently a search was on. It was only a matter of hours before it would intensify. I gathered up a few notes and files, and cast a quick glance up to pay my respects to the ghosts of township residents long departed who breathed, struggled, and cast votes in this place. Also on my mind were the residents who died here during the Spanish Flu epidemic, when the hall was used as a makeshift hospital.

It was time to go; I crossed quickly to Marge's car, slid in the front passenger seat, and glanced about as she also stepped into the vehicle. My knapsack was in my lap.

"Do you want me to take you to L'Anse?"

"Can I just borrow your car and drop it home?"

I needed to get to the County Courthouse Annex or the Historical Society Museum in Baraga and look through some records. A vague idea was forming in my mind, blurred with the blows and fatigue of the day. Adrenaline was coursing now, sharpening what few vital instincts remained. I needed to survive.

Her last words before getting out were: "You damned car thief," followed by a slight smile. "Good luck, Conn. Sorry about trying to take off your head."

I drove off, torn between connecting the remaining threads and escape from the township. L'Anse would bring me law enforcement, who I wasn't sure was all clean. My hospital experience and escape told me that.

Inching out of her driveway on M-38, I stopped to let on oncoming semi-tractor drive past. I saw a flash of recognition from the driver as he looked down from his high cockpit in the red beast. My decision was made for me, run for the hills.

I squealed out onto the pavement, seeing the semi pull off onto the shoulder a half-mile west, a cloud of dust marking his stopping point. I hammered the accelerator and sped away past him.

I was doing 85, and the semi-tractor was bearing down on me from behind. I couldn't coax much more out of the small four-cylinder wagon. The massive silver grille filled the rearview mirror, and the impact of the rampaging monster nearly drove the car off the road. I swerved into the oncoming lane to regain control, tires screaming and smoking. The other driver was maneuvering to finish me off, and it would be easily done. I fishtailed into the high grass off the shoulder, dirt spraying around me. The truck likewise swirled in smoke as the beast spat fire and plumes of dust across the road, trying to stop.

The steering and rear-end felt damaged, but I wrenched the wheel and got back on M-38. Another vehicle suddenly veered toward me. I spun the wheel to take the impact again into the rear of the car and braced for the impact. It came in a swirling maelstrom of screaming metal. My vehicle, impaled on the front of the huge blue pickup, was being carried into the field, slowed by the wet clay of the recently turned up field.

Slamming to a stop, I elbowed the door open, having difficulty as the frame of the car twisted and turned under the side loading and fell out into the soft mud. The driver of the pickup leered at me, and slowly climbed out of his truck with his pistol hanging negligently by his side. I was a wolf at bay — a pup. I did not have anywhere to run and would have lacked the strength to do so even if there was a place.

"OK, Hotshot, now you die," a voice said. "I am going to enjoy this. I don't even think you remember me, do you?"

Frank Riley. He was a tatted-up brute, knotted muscles curling up at his neck.

"Still selling drugs, Frankie?" I asked. "How much child support do you pay a month, knocking up addicts?" I needed to make him mad. A marginally in-control Frank might put a bullet straight through my heart and I needed him off-balance.

His face grew red. Fangs appeared, I noticed quite a few broken and blackened from drug use.

He stopped and considered me from heavy-lidded eyes. As he lifted his gun, I caught a glint of metal and studied the approach of the semi driver. I recognized him — he was from

Baraga, and I thought his name was Tommy. He lifted a hand as he approached Frankie.

"Shoot him in the leg, we need him alive. We don't know who he has talked to."

Frankie considered this, scratching the side of his head with the pistol. Mental mustache-twirling, I guess.

I stared at Frankie and lifted my chin. No running, no crying, no whimpering. He didn't like that.

"On your knees, Connie-boy. Let's hear more of that smart talk before you bleed all over this here dirt. You always thought you were better than me, Connie."

"It didn't take too much thought and effort to actually be better, either, Frankie."

He had beaten up a girl in our high-school class, right after lunch in a classroom after she told him she might be pregnant. She lost the baby and missed a year of school. Frankie also beat down our civics teacher who tried to intervene. It took me and two other guys to restrain him. He served a year in juvie after that. I had moved out of the area; this was my first time seeing him after all these years.

"Sure you can even shoot straight, all hopped up on drugs, Frankie? You don't look so well. Jumpy. How is that meth? Mix well with the booze and woman-beating booster shots?"

He erupted, his pistol flying out in front of him. I dove to the side, and then rolled behind the destroyed Subaru. He screamed my name, and shots flashed into the car, which shuddered under the impacts of what must have been at least .357 rounds.

Chapter 28

I had one foot mired in the clay next to a tire and pulled it free just as Frankie stepped around the grille. His blackened smile grew wide, lips pulled back in an animal gaze. The hunter and the hunted. The hammer pulled back on the double-action weapon.

The rifle shot echoed across the open field, reverberating off the woods enclosing the north end. Frankie stared wide-eyed at me, trying to train the weapon on me, but someone was losing some coordination. It may have been the shattered torso. The rifled slug had taken out a large portion of his right side and blood poured from his plaid shirt. His eyes rolled back, and he collapsed not three feet from me. I put a heavy boot down on his gun-hand and another swung at his face, connecting with the soft tissue. His scream rent the acrid air and it too echoed in the field.

Then all was silence, except for his moans, the hissing of exploded tires, and the shattered wreck of the car.

I slowly came up to see a group of four sheriff's deputies carefully moving across the field in formation, rifles at their shoulders, all trained on Tommy, who stood with his hands up.

Officer Anderson stood a short distance away from me, a hand half-lifted to her men and also greeting me. She seemed to soften when seeing me, but perhaps I imagined that.

"When you called, we expected you to wait at the Alston Town Hall, Conn," she said.

"Was it hard to miss the action here, on your way?"

"A call wouldn't have hurt, Conn. We are here to protect and serve. Also save your sorry ass, it appears."

I looked around at the assembled party, all in bulletproof vests and tactical gear.

"I have the MSP Heavy Team out of Negaunee on its way, too."

It started with the roaring of heavy wings and a whirl of dust and vapor as a helicopter flashed down out of the blue skies. The officers shielded their eyes against the sun and the vortex of wind. The air felt like a hive had broken open, and swarms of bees were tumbling out of the sky.

As Officer Anderson grinned, the expression solidified into shock as her right shoulder jerked back, and the phfittt of an unseen bullet reported across the field. The air swarmed with more of the buzzing. A marksman was leaning out the passenger side cargo door and aiming a rifle. Whoever it was, they were good. The officers around me went down like carnival toy targets. The shooter was going for the biggest stuffed animal he could win.

One officer was down on one knee, firing up into the fury. A small grey puff appeared on the fuselage, the chopper waggled, then peeled away. The officer half-rose and put a shot into the little semi-driver, who rose from behind my wrecked car with a pistol. The little man flew backwards, nearly theatrically. Not to be outdone, I put a boot into Frankie, who was semi-conscious and trying to lift his pistol.

I recognized Stone Face who reached for a black handset on his upper left shoulder, and I heard the crackle as the respondent came to life. I heard, "Four men down, M-38, two miles west of the airport." I guess Officer Anderson was one of the guys. I knelt beside her and she gripped my arm. I ripped off my jacket and covered the wound on her shoulder. "Looks like he got you right at the strap, just under the vest," she said.

"Lucky shot." She tried to sit up. "What about Lou, Steve, and Paul?"

Stone Face yelled from 100 feet away: "Lou is okay, Paul is out." Apparently, Stone Face was Steve. "They will live, but Paul needs attention fast. The cavalry is on its way."

I pushed her gently back to the ground; she was struggling to sit upright. I bundled the jacket behind her head, draping one sleeve over her shoulder, pressing her hand to it. "Keep pressure on it." I got up and went to Lou, who I had figured out by process of elimination. I am pretty sharp.

Stone Face was right; Lou had taken a shot to his thigh. He waved me off. "I am okay. Who the hell was that?" He looked at me with red-rimmed eyes. "What kind of trouble are you into?"

"I wish I knew. Truly"

Chapter 29

The tactical team showed up 10 minutes later, along with three ambulances. The gleaming white vehicles proclaimed "Bay Ambulance," and orange–coated EMTs poured out. Pretty impressive. The TAC team was headed by a clean-shaven and hard-faced man of around 50. He looked around grimly and shook his head slowly. The side-long look he gave me while speaking to Officer Anderson was not one of gentle curiosity. It had probably been a while since automatic weapons and helicopter gun battles had occurred in Upper Michigan.

I rode with him and two other troopers in one of the suburbans. Not in the front — I wasn't afforded that privilege. They really wanted to look in the bag I had retrieved from the Subaru, but I clutched it to me.

On the way back to Baraga County Memorial, the team kept their silence. We met numerous vehicles of various blackened persuasions. Where on Earth did all these people come from? I was impressed.

They escorted me into an examining room, and a hand wave dedicated a guard to me. A nurse practitioner attended to various wounds all over my body. I now understood the oft-repeated cliché of "tsk, tsk." She worked wordlessly, which made me wonder if she had combat experience. I caught a glimpse of myself in a small mirror in the room and mentally recoiled at the battered, bruised, scratched, clawed, and generally beat-up mess that stared back at me. I passed out.

***

I awoke, feeling the sensation of a warm and gentle scrubbing. I was lying down while a male and female attendant cleaned my wounds with sponges. "I hardly know you guys; can't you buy me a drink first?" The two tried hard not to crack a smile.

"Do you ever shut up?" A female voice from behind the curtain. One of my attendants pulled it back. Officer Anderson looked pretty well for having just been shot, and was laying in a hospital gown in the other bed in the suite.

"Hey, this isn't a co-ed room," I prodded.

She rolled her eyes at me.

"I asked to share the room so we could talk." She swung her head, dismissing the attendants.

"Hey, that felt great, I protest!"

Again, the eye rolling.

She relented and told them to come back in an hour. "He needs a shower, at least four of them."

She leveled her gaze, and I leaned back, desperate to sleep again. "Anyone attacking me tonight? If so, I need another escape route. You can't use the same one twice."

She wasn't rolling her eyes now, and looked a bit ticked off.

Good, I thought. That makes quite a few of us.

"Conn, there is a trail of bodies, explosions, shootings, and crashes stretching out for 20 miles west from here to Alston. I need to hear everything. You are still under suspicion for the murder charges, especially when you escaped. You have somehow escaped from two dragnets: law enforcement and whoever is after you."

I closed my eyes as she explained that there had been a well-coordinated manhunt over the past 36 hours, hence the stream of law enforcement vehicles. Teams had driven or flown in from Lansing, Minneapolis, and Duluth. I was impressed again, and told her: "Aw shucks. . ."

Her sharp intake of breath told me she was reaching a limit with my wisecracks, so I kept momentarily silent.

"Do you trust me, Conn?" she asked after a pause.

"How is my dog?" I demurred.

"Missing you. He lies by the door and whines. He has scratched up my front door and torn carpet up near the entry. Loyalty?"

"He is just crazy."

She softened at that. "You owe me some home renovation costs after this."

"Oh really? I haven't felt like there will be an 'after this' over the past few days."

"Reach back under your pillow."

I gave her a questioning look, but a flick of her chin prompted me to reach back. It hurt to even do that. Geez.

My bag. It was there tucked away.

"Now check the other side," she said. I palmed around, twisting my shoulder. I felt the cool steel handle and caressed the barrel.

My 9. I was impressed again. I hoped my face did not betray me.

"Safety is off," she said.

I did smile a bit.

"Please talk," she said. "It's just you and I. By the way, Davey's wife hasn't pressed charges yet."

That was something, but really the least of my worries. I told her everything. Well, almost. My escape, my house, the ambush shootings, Susan and her killing, the explosions, the town hall . . . I left out the part about my aunt, since I had a feeling she was already in deep trouble with whomever she and fancy boy were tied up with.

"Marge was kidnapped, and I stole her car," I continued. "I jumped her in the town hall."

She laughed. "We just talked to her. Sounds like she ambushed you and lent you her car. You escape a dozen killers, a car chase, hunter helicopters, and an old lady with a snow shovel is what nearly takes you out."

I had to smile also. "She didn't 'take me out.' I was weak from loss of blood."

Her eyes had warmth and a depth to them. I decided then I could trust her. Mostly. I also didn't mention the other call I I made from the town hall.

She noticed me glancing at the hall.

"Steve is covering the shift tonight," she said. "Nothing will happen to us."

"Did you find out who attacked me in here?" I asked. "Which officer let him in?"

"The cameras showed a man in a hoodie. No definitive facial recognition. The officer was a trainee from downstate, turns out he has an interesting family history and some questionable ties to some bad characters that didn't show up on screening. He simply walked away from his post guarding you.

"Parking lot cameras?"

"Nothing. Blacked out plate on the assailant's vehicle. Probably one of your friends out in Alston."

I didn't quite snort, but it came out as a bit of one. More of a cough.

"You look like hell, Conn," she said. A partial grin tugged at one corner of her mouth. She had really cute dimples. And a dusting of freckles.

"Gee, thanks. My stylist and personal team of attendants and makeup artists should be here soon, so we will take care of that."

My attendants came to help me into a shower again. No way. I tripped and stumbled to the bathroom and fell into the stall. The warm water felt amazing. I was ready to sleep standing up. Some food and sleep. Tomorrow . . .

After the shower, I returned to my bed. As I drifted off, I heard Officer Anderson murmur across the room: "We are going for a ride."

Chapter 30

Officer Anderson, who I was now in the habit of calling Bella, and I left the following day — a Saturday — in her Jeep Wrangler. We drove down US-41, and I asked her to stop at the Evergreen Cemetery in L'Anse. We turned in and I had to get my bearings. It had taken me a while in previous years to find the grave of Henry Laird. I knew it was up and to the left of the entrance on the north side of the gently rolling acreage.

Finding the grave, I pointed out the unusual headstones of Henry Laird and James Kyle, which were atypical for Union veterans. I had viewed thousands of typical Union veteran headstones, most commissioned by the Grand Army of The Republic, essentially a veterans' organization similar to the American Legion of today. These headstones usually were three-foot slabs of white rock, with a semi-circular top. James and Henry's were long, tapered affairs, ornamented at the top with a small lantern-looking headpiece. Henry's had broken off and was lying in the grass next to the grave.

"I came here with another historian and a ground-penetrating radar team from Michigan Tech University, trying to ascertain if there were really two graves down there," I said to Bella. "The results were somewhat inconclusive, but it sure seemed like the graves were dug together, and if there are two bodies, they were laid side-by-side, even though they died years apart."

I pointed to the inscription on Henry's stone. "Company D, New York. That's where the problem for me started." I explained to Bella the mystery surrounding Laird's service and the contradicting depictions on his headstone.

I gazed around the small cemetery, peaceful in the filtered morning light. I then set out, telling Bella to look for the name Carlyle. "It could be spelled a couple different ways. I am looking for late 1800s to 1920s vintage, probably listed as a pastor or reverend."

It took over an hour, but we did find it between a Charlotte Brown and an Irving M. Waiting, with an inscription "Rarely Hid In." It wasn't all that far from Henry's, in the older downhill portion of the plot.

Rev. Joshua Carlyle
Methodist
1860-1915
Proverbs 2:4

We circled the grave, and Bella knelt at the gravestone, pulling away some grass at the base and clawing away some loose dirt. She stood with some streamers or fragments of red cloth, edged with white.

"Looks like someone had placed an American flag decades ago," she said. "It has since rotted away."

I took them from her. "No, look . . ." I laid them out on the ground and drew a gasp from her.

We could see the rough outline of the Stars and Bars. A Confederate flag.

We stood for a moment in silence, and then she knelt again. There was another inscription lower down, half buried in soil, and grimy. She walked over to her Jeep and got a bottle of water, which she splashed on the face. A minute of rubbing, and she stood and smiled. "Another Bible verse. Job 28: 1-4."

"Could I see your phone, please?"

I ran a search for the verses on her smartphone and smiled grimly as I read the results. "Job 28: 1. Surely there is a mine for silver and a place where they refine gold. He sinks a shaft far from habitation, forgotten by the foot."

I did another search.

"Proverbs 2: 4 reads 'If you seek her as silver and search for her as hidden treasures.' I think we found the right gravestone."

"That's incredible, Conn."

"This only raises another question," I said. "Carlyle was a Methodist preacher in Alston, who moved along with his church to L'Anse. The church burned in the 1980s, and whatever clues were there disappeared."

She smiled. "Are there any Carlyles in L'Anse?"

"I don't know, but we can find out."

We next stopped along the water at the head of Keweenaw Bay, halfway between L'Anse and Baraga. The expanse of water opened up to the north, while the circumference of the bay swept in either direction. It was a beautiful fall day; seagulls swooped down from cloudless blue skies, moving seemingly against the chill of the fall morning. I breathed deeply, refreshed as always by the beautiful panorama. I climbed reluctantly back into the vehicle. Our second stop for the morning was at the Baraga County Historical Museum across the bay.

As we opened our doors, we glanced at each other, knowing wordlessly we still had an antagonist at large who had large resources at his disposal. We would gain nothing by hiding. I squeezed her hand by way of thanks.

"They shot at me, too, Conn," she said. "This is personal."

"We also sent officers to your aunt's. They have disappeared. There is an APB out on them now. We also have Steve leading a team investigating who your friends work for. Hopefully we get leads by tomorrow. No sign of the men who were pursuing you. The Haakanen brothers also disappeared. Someone is doing some pre-emptive cleanup, keeping us all in the dark."

We both felt our only way out was to solve what we could of the mystery. We had today and tomorrow to possibly to track down the clues, knowing the risks that were still out there stalking us. It was sobering.

I stood outside for a moment, looking up at the sun. Bella cast an inquiring glance at me. Something nagged at the back of my mind, and again the tiles started clicking into places.

***

155

Brenda Petersen, a striking brunette who I went to high school with, was working at the museum, and she gave me a quick smile when I walked in. "Well, Conn, I do believe it has been a while. My God, what happened to your face?"

Brenda had long hair, pulled back loosely in a ponytail. She was tall and curvy, and her thicker, black-rimmed glasses only added to her scholarly appearance.

"Hunting accident, Brenda. I was hunting for my TV remote and tangled with the Laz-Z-Boy"

"Looks like it won, if you don't mind me saying, Conn." She took the sting out of her words with a smile.

Bella 'ahem-ed' impatiently. Maybe it was my imagination, but was it a bit of jealousy?

"You might be right," I said. I could feel my driver rolling her eyes behind me.

"What do you have as far as maps from the 1800s here? Anything from the mission in Keweenaw Bay?"

"Conn, we have a few older railroad maps from the 1880s and 1890s. What years are you looking for?"

"As early as possible. 1860s would work also."

She walked over to a set of long and flat wooden drawers and pulled out a few large sheets of paper.

Bella was impatient. "Why are we looking at old maps?"

"They might contain a clue as to why people are shooting at us."

"OK, what are we looking for? You mentioned a mission?"

"There was a Catholic Mission in Keweenaw Bay that worked with the Ojibwa and local miners, merchants, and

156

traders. They were served by a Slovenian priest who spoke eight languages. Pretty amazing guy. He also worked to develop a written version and dictionary of the Ojibwa language, which was cool but not used today. Mainly a historic text."

"I know that Bishop Baraga served here," she said. "The Snowshoe Priest. I drive by his statue every time I drive down this way. What does he have to do with us?"

"I think he had a conversation with an important individual in this story." Even as I said this, I heard a distant chord of dissent strike in my own mind.

I scanned through a few maps, finally pulling one out and laying it on top of the small pile, holding down the edges with my fingertips. It was a rough old logging map, dated 1880. It was of Baraga County. There were a few logging railroads inked in, and a few dotted lines indicating main logging routes.

Many of the main logging routes became portions of the main highways of the present day. I placed a forefinger on the map, along a river. I traced its path and found the confluence of another.

I looked up from my study of the map, and Brenda gave me a quizzical half-smile. "Brenda, would you have any records of the staff at the Assinnins mission who worked with Bishop Baraga?"

"I don't think so, but the Diocese might in Marquette. I can make a few calls. Anyone in particular?"

"I was given the name of a native woman — Susan — serving in 1863." Brenda walked into her office, and I could see her dialing through the glass on her door.

"We need to take a drive and then a hike." I told Bella.

Brenda came back and said, "They will get back to me. I can call you once I get some information."

I asked Bella to give her a cell number and thanked her profusely. I got a warm and beautiful smile in return. Bella didn't kick me but gave me a push out the door. Philistine, no respect for scholarly endeavors.

"Brenda, do you have any records for a Carlyle family here in Baraga or L'Anse?" Brenda frowned and walked back into her office. I could see her at her computer. She called out: "I am looking on a few genealogical sites we have access to. What years?"

I gave her the dates, and she said: "Nothing. He was never married, no known heirs."

It was my turn to frown. "Any sisters or brothers?"

"Yes. One sister. Sally McAllister." I walked into her office and leaned over her shoulder. She leaned back.

"Alston, Michigan." I raised an eyebrow. Current descendants?"

She tapped out a few letters. "Yes, Margaret Moray, née Kasperanen"

I think my face registered my shock. Marge. The Laird Township Treasurer whose vehicle I just wrecked.

"Brenda, you are amazing." She looked up and said: "I assume you will come back and buy me dinner in thanks? Maybe explain what all this is about?"

"Absolutely."

Bella took the lead out the door. Maybe there was some professional jealousy. Such is the exciting life of an amateur researcher and object of a manhunt.

A few bottles of water, some sandwiches, and sundries from the market across the road, and we were off, heading west on M-38. We slowed briefly at the scene of the events of the past week. Only rutted tire tracks remained of the confrontation. We both cast glances up in the sky.

Bella commented. "I called a few friends at the FAA; no records of the helicopter exist. Even the private ones are supposed to file a flight plan. I am guessing they are located within a hundred miles, which would give them 20 minutes to find you."

That got an "hmm" from me, and she gave me a sideways glance. "You are pretty calm for a sitting duck. Or a decoy duck, as the case may be. Someone knows we are in this vehicle. My department is obviously infiltrated; we may as well paint an X on the roof."

"Someone probably has." My black humor surfacing.

But it wasn't far off.

The sun was moving overhead, off to our south, with the late October sun making its daily transit lower and lower along the horizon. Then we heard it again — the far-off buzz.

"My God," she pointed. A chopper dropped a mile in front

of us, hovering less than 500 feet over the highway, sunlight glinting off its dark hull and windscreen.

"Evasive action is called for, I believe," I said.

She nodded and cranked the wheel left, and we shuddered around a corner onto Prickett Dam Road, heading south in a cloud of dust and gravel. The helicopter changed direction and kept pace along the treetops, dipping, and swooping like an angry wasp, lofting left and right, angling in pursuit.

I reached in the backseat for some of the gear we brought along. Bella really had a nice personal collection of rifles. I admired one in my lap and affixed a scope as we raced along.

We crested a hill, and breathing heavily, Bella pointed to the right, in advance of the road turning west towards the Prickett Dam access road. I waved her off and gave her a chopping motion straight ahead towards the dam. She gaped, but continued ahead, slowing as we approached the small parking lot at the bottom of the hill.

"Great, now we are trapped," she said.

"Oh ye of little faith."

The helicopter circled slowly, like a lion stalking its prey. It drifted off to the southeast, slewing sideways. We could see a door slide open from our parked position.

"Let's get out of here!" Bella reached for the shifter, and I stopped her with a hand. "Conn, What!?"

We could see a rifleman taking aim out of the window. We both caught our breath. She grabbed my wrist to remove it from her hand.

A fiery streak rose from the top of the dam. It angled along the low horizon and ended at the helicopter. The explosion was a thunderclap of sound in the confines of the Sturgeon River Valley that echoed across the lake and forests. A brilliant red and yellow shower shone starkly against the blue of the morning sky.

"Son of a…" she punched my arm. A few more profanities resounded in the confines of the cab, and then she got out, slammed the door and for all intents, stomped around the perimeter of the lot.

I got out of the passenger side and raised a hand to two figures that appeared on the top of the dam. I could barely make out the silhouette of a small tube in the hand of one figure. I could make out a "V" sign from the other figure. Either that was 'victory' or they had another rocket launcher at hand, ready for a second shot. I raised a fist, and then thumped it across my chest. A bit of macho posturing, but damn. That was glorious. Or was it "dam"? I was good with them both.

Bella was really mad, and she walked away along an access road that curved around to the dam. I hopped in the driver's seat, started the engine, and coasted up alongside her. She jutted her chin out and pointedly ignored me.

"Oh, c'mon. You said yourself we were decoys."

A glare, stony silence, she kept walking.

"How about a nice cool drink of water? Maybe you want push me in the water?"

"Don't resurface if you do."

My goodness. She was walking up the slight rise to the wing wall of the dam. I put the Jeep into park and got out.

"We aren't speaking to them," I said. "That will be later." She shaded her eyes against the sun. "Who are they?"

"The cavalry."

She spun on me, stepped over and pounded my chest lightly with both fists.

"Hey!" I said.

Then she hugged me and buried her face in my chest briefly.

She let me drive.

Chapter 31

I took the gravel road towards the boat landing. 10 minutes later, we were at the foot of Silver Mountain. It was time for a little exploration.

Opening the rear hatch, Bella and I wordlessly strapped on small packs and slung AR-15s over our shoulders. As I noted, she had a nice collection of firearms. We both grabbed a few magazines and then reached in for a few more. We had seen the face of a small war; hopefully we would be prepared somewhat for the next round.

"I want to hear about your friends on the dam someday and why they thought we'd meet them there," Bella's words almost spat out. "We could've died if you were off on your timing."

"Dedication and deduction."

"Don't forget decoys and dummies." She set off towards the woods. Not quite stomping off, but close.

"Don't you want to know where we are going?" I asked. "Or looking for?"

"Bad guys, treasure, secrets, answers." Now she was verbally rolling her eyes. This was going to be fun.

"Who is the hell has friends with rocket launchers?" she continued. It felt rhetorical from her.

Who doesn't? I owed Caleb and Gene.

"Let me know when you find all those answers," I said. "I will be here with a few of the clues if you would care to listen in." I leaned back against the Jeep and attempted to nonchalantly whistle, but my lips were too bruised and broken to pull it off. I kind of coughed, but hoped I looked cool doing it.

She came back, crossed her arms in front of her, and stood in front of me. Without smiling.

"A Confederate soldier in 1863 was making his way north with two wagons and three other guys," I explained. "Somewhere on what would become the military road the following year, they got into a gunfight along a river crossing and one of the wagons was lost. The soldier indicated that they had been travelling for two weeks from southern Indiana, so that puts the shootout at least in northern Wisconsin."

"Can I ask why we didn't go check the wreckage of the helicopter?" Bella interrupted.

"Because the helicopter crashed on the shore of the lake which is hard to get to. There was nothing left, and they tried to kill us. Twice. Gene and Caleb will confirm."

At the drop of the names, she just started at me. She went to speak, and now I interrupted. "Plus there may be more on the way, and the faster we get to the bottom of this, the faster we can bring some sort of resolution to the issue." I wished I felt as confident as I sounded. The tiles in my mind were clicking; pieces were dropping into some semblance of place and I wanted to see this through.

"If they stayed on the military road following the gunfight, masquerading as Union troops, two weeks at 25-30 miles per day would put them near Upper Michigan," I said. "There are a lot of streams, but only a few major rivers. Our mystery man also mentioned running into miners, which puts them up in this area, if not further north."

I took a quick drink of water and scanned the surroundings. With most of the leaves fallen or nearly so, we had a clear view of the base of Silver Mountain. I strongly felt most of my answers lay here or within a few miles. Maples, pine, and birch constituted most of the trees in the area. A few dark green hemlocks dotted the north side of the hummock. All of the stories, along with the diary entry, pointed to something in the area.

The mountain used to have 260-something stairs to the top, but they had been removed recently. The old creosote-coated timber steps had originally been built in the 1930s by the Civilian Conservation Corps, which had worked on many public recreation projects as part of the New Deal. The "mountain" really was a low-rising piece of ground of just over a few hundred feet, but the views from the top of the basalt upthrust were really something.

"And you are picking this location because?" Bella moved up beside me on the trail.

"Because entries in his diary indicate a mission on Lake Superior, and also passing some chalky cliffs which could be here or along the Silver, Ontonagon, or Sturgeon Rivers. He was most likely headed east from the river, which I believe was the Ontonagon River, on what is now Military Hill. I think the wagon is here. The name Silver Mountain predates the Civil War, but wouldn't that be something if there was a wagon lodged in there with something of value?"

I continued. "There was an old Indian trail going through here to L'Anse, with a leg that went up to Keweenaw Bay to the Catholic Mission. If the soldiers had continued up what is now M-26 on the military and mining road, there was also a leg that swung down though Twin Lakes, north of Alston, heading east by southeast, also and ultimately to the Mission. We might be hard pressed to find chalky cliffs along that route, but there are some."

"And you think the treasure cave is just sitting out here in broad daylight? Untouched for 150 plus years?" She didn't have to roll her eyes, the implication was clear.

"I think we can find some evidence of an old rock fall, maybe caused by a blast. This area has also had rumors of a Great Spirit that guards the mountain. Maybe our solider started the rumor whilst convalescing in an Indian Mission, to keep people away from it."

We made our way along the southern face of the cliffs. I was surveying our surroundings, rather than at the yellowed basalt walls. I was trying to pick out a 150-year old trail and the trees that would have defined that path. The trail would have led to higher ground and wound in from the Sturgeon River to our south and east. I could vaguely pick out a few possible routes.

We stopped at a pile of rock, eroded from the face, and

scanned its white surface.

"Let's keep walking," I said. "I assumed he came in from the south or southeast along the river, but he could've come in from the west or northwest."

We spent the next hour making a circuit of the mountain, pausing briefly as I scanned a rock fall that cascaded down into a wash-out. I briefly considered the location, not sure the ravine or gully could have formed in the last 150 years, as it would make the approach of a wagon impossible. The size of the trees along the edge of the ravine also could preclude a former road coming around or into this side of the mountain.

Bella was checking her phone and trying to call up the map function, but couldn't get any signal. I pulled a small paper map out of my jacket pocket and held it out of the shadow of my body.

I spoke as I scanned the map. "In 1844, prospectors and surveyors took note of 'gray sulphuret of copper,' most likely sulfur, along a vein on the east face of the mountain. This offered a faint promise of silver being present, so the National Mining Company of Pontiac was formed: six gentlemen plus a guy from Detroit named Gillett, who would become Jacob Houghton's father-in-law."

Bella arched her eyebrow at the Houghton name.

"In 1845, the National crew drove a horizontal shaft 140 feet into the mountain, following the gray sulfide, and they sank an additional vertical shaft down from there to see if the vein spread out. They found nothing. The National's mining actually came to an end not because of the poor prospects, but a tragedy on Lake Superior." I paused to remember. "A schooner by the name of Merchant left from Sault Ste. Marie on June 12, 1847, headed for the Copper Country. A number of passengers were miners from the National Company heading to Silver Mountain, including two guys from Pontiac, and two from Ohio. One day out from Sault Ste. Marie, a huge storm took the ship to the depths of the Lake. Nothing was ever found of the ship besides a hatch that washed up on a beach in Ontario."

Her eyes widened as I continued. "The supposed curse surrounding this place was only compounded by another unusual 'shipwreck.' The National operation was shut down after the first disaster, and 'wreckers' came to haul away any remains of the operation. Everything got loaded on a raft, and floated down the Sturgeon River, right down there, to the Copper Country. As the raft entered Otter Lake, 10 or so miles from here, another storm came up, and the raft broke apart, sinking with its cargo: irons, forge, blower, anvils, blacksmith tools, and the like."

I continued. "So basically, two shipwrecks doomed the operation, giving credence to the story of the Great Spirit guarding the mountain." I took a drink of water. "A man by the name of Everett from Marquette bought the mountain in 1864 but never did anything with it. Then, in the 1880s, Orrin Robinson, of the Sturgeon River Lumber Company fame in Hancock and Chassell, bought the mountain property and formed a mining operation with some gentlemen from Hancock and Houghton, including prominent men such as

E.L. Wright, Edward Ryan, and William Condon. This new Silver Mountain Mining Company sent out a team under William Davis to explore the holdings at the mine. After two weeks, nothing was found to indicate any prospects, so the operation folded up."

Bella was getting bored by my narrative, but I pressed on. "This also seems strange to me, because in his autobiography, Orrin mentioned that nothing was found there and that the Alston brothers snooped around after he did." I paused myself, thinking that indeed maybe the Alstons were after the prospect of silver and the treasure. I finished my long-winded exposition. "But why would Orrin not only buy the property, but form an actual company with some heavy hitters, and then go exploring?"

She was rolling her eyes and interjected. "So where does that lead us? Where do you want to go now?"

"Can we stop and see my dog?"

"If you are a good boy, we will."

Sigh. "Should've picked him up, he would love being out here."

"Sure, then he could be part of our day of fun, chasing rockets, dodging bullets, exploding mine shafts . . ."

My, she was spending too much time with me. Is sarcasm contagious?

I couldn't spot anything else and was thinking we should head into Ontonagon County. Our mystery man could've pulled up to some of the bluffs if he headed west from the mining road. There was a road along the base of the cliffs headed towards Rockland, where US-45 intersected M-26 and swung west. I guess it would just be a day of hiking.

I thought about what I knew about the Catholic Mission in Assinins. I remember reading Lady Unafraid about a young girl named Rebecca Jewel Francis who served as a missionary teacher across the bay in L'Anse, for the Methodist Mission. There it was. Click. And another. Carlyle and Methodists. From what I knew, there was some competition across the bays between the missions, each trying to win converts and proud of their relationships with the Native peoples in the area.

Something was nagging at me about these missions. I wonder if Mr. Carlyle was visiting Mr. Baraga at any time and hearing about the soldier's story? No, wait, he would've appeared on the scene decades later.

Bella stopped ahead of me and turned. "What?"

I guess maybe she should know more of the story. I related the story of the convalescence of the mystery solder —the first to record his story in the old book I'd been carrying with me. I already guessed that when the soldier related that it cost a "King's Ransom" to stay, it was a play on the Ransom Sheldon name in Houghton. Ransom was off serving in the Union army, so a member of his family or a relative may have sheltered this confederate soldier at the price of his last remaining silver coin. Ransom Sheldon served with the 'Houghton Regiment' in the 22nd Michigan. It wouldn't have gone over too well in these parts, having sheltered a Southern soldier, so I'm guessing he kept this a secret. He mentioned his accent in the diary.

The diary. It was time to read more. I did not want to in the hospital, risking drifting off and having it stolen from my hands. I sat on a small rock outcropping along the western escarpment base and took the book from my backpack.

Bella dropped next to me and opened a bottle of water. "Is that the magic source of all of your knowledge?"

I nodded. "Some of it."

Chapter 32

The second set of handwriting in the diary had been only a short paragraph. Now I flipped through the pages and saw that the third set of writing took up another dozen or so pages and left the balance of the book blank. The remaining empty pages had small markings in the upper corners, but were otherwise bereft of script.

December, 1907

I too take pen in hand to document the search for what I can only assume is something worth dying to protect. Maybe not just dying, but willing to kill to for. I have chosen to write these words to commemorate the life of a fine man who saved my life."

I noticed Bella was leaning over my shoulder, reading. We looked at each other and returned to the book. The pages opened up:

I was kidnapped and held by an evil man by the name of Felix and forced to . . . do things . . . with men who paid him to have their way with me. I was chained in the back lean-to of a shack, with another girl in an adjacent room. Horrible things happened there that I will not relate, nor is it profitable to do so and thus relive the darkest period of my life. I will relate rather the incredible destructive power of my rescuer, who appeared one day in righteous fury as our salvation.

I heard a tremendous crash, shouts, and gunshots. My door was smashed open, and my tormenter flew on his back into the room, landing on the remnants of the wooden slab that had served as my prison cell door. Felix flailed about helplessly on the floor as I recoiled in the corner of my bed, clutching the rag remnants of what once had been blankets.

I will never forget my rescuer's fury. He was dressed all in black, blood dripping from his fists, and his eyes — deep-set, dark, full of righteous fire, and red-rimmed with terrible power and knowledge. His glance caught mine, and he reached for a pistol from his waistband and fired two shots into Felix, one in each knee. He stepped out, and I heard the other door smash open, and again the yells of rage and blows, and he came back to me. With infinite gentleness, he undid my bonds and carried me outside, laying me gently on the tall grass underneath a tree that I had only seen small glimpses of. It was a giant pine, with outstretched branches that seemed to embrace the sky. I had called it my "Praying Tree" and indeed that day my prayers were answered.

I looked up, my focus catching the rays of sunlight streaming through the branches and wisps of steam that rose from the earth around me as the world warmed to its touch. I closed my eyes and breathed deeply and started to weep. I tried to rise and stumbled, but made my way to my fellow captive.

She bore the scars of having been badly beaten, and she too wept, and we held on to each other, closing our eyes and rocking back and forth. We shut out the sounds around us, secure in the knowledge of rescue and salvation.

The sounds around us faded away, and our rescuer came over and knelt beside us, speaking for the first time. He caressed the girl's cheek and spoke in quiet tones, and I heard the name "Cassie." She looked up, incredulous, reached out her arms weakly, and they fell into each other, both crying openly, and she buried her face in his chest.

It was her uncle, and he had been looking for her for months, going from settlement to settlement, from mining camps to lumber mills and railroad towns, and everywhere in between throughout Indiana, Wisconsin, and Michigan. He had followed whispers and rumors and seen unspeakable things. He had found her sister's body in northern Wisconsin, and buried her somewhere near a border town.

My rescuer's name was Ezekiel, and he had followed Cassie into this wilderness and would have followed her unto the ends of the Earth, though indeed this place felt like it was the end of the Earth already. I should mention that it was much later I learned Ezekiel was his late brother's name, and he had taken the moniker upon himself to honor his brother's legacy, vowing to find his daughters.

We drove away from that place, and I cast one glance back

to see the shack and outbuildings in flames. The bodies of the three men had been stood against the pine trees in the yard and bound with rope. All three had their hands spiked together above their heads, crucified in grotesque fashion. A plank had been branded with lettering, and I could make out the word and numbers even from a great distance. The plank had been nailed above Felix's head:

Ezekiel 25:17.

I will never forget that verse. I looked it up weeks later:

"And I will execute great vengeance upon this with furious rebukes, and they shall know that I am the Lord, when I shall lay my vengeance upon them."

We were taken on a short ride to the small logging and railroad town of Alston. I shuddered when we rode past the mill and I heard the starting whistle, the same one that had portended my horrific experiences until now. Surely some of the men that came to me worked here — even the two that died in that place.

A doctor came by train the next morning and attended to us. I believe his name was Hanna. We were given rooms in Willette's Boarding House and cared for very well.

My family came down to get me from Houghton. I had been imprisoned only 30 miles from where I was taken, and that bitterness stayed with me. My father had hired *investigators who had ranged throughout the Great Lakes and assumed I had been taken by ship to points unknown. I later learned that the cost of the search had nearly bankrupted my father.*

My family's joy was unbounded, exceeded only by my own. I returned to Houghton, having persuaded Cassie and her uncle to stay with us until she rested and recuperated.

Ezekiel would hardly sleep, his search had consumed him, and we found him often in front of the fire late at night, or walking around outside our home on the Avenue, watching the house and surroundings. My father had close friends over, including Ransom Sheldon, Jr., and inquired of our guest's past. Ezekiel politely demurred, always deferring questions about his time in the military.

One dark and rainy night, I heard low voices in the parlor, and unable to sleep, came partway down the grand stairs to overhear a group of men talking. I heard Ezekiel's name spoken, a rumbling of argument, and then my father say: "We know nothing about him, but I am sure I saw him in the war."

Another said: "That was nearly 40 years ago, how can you trust your memory?"

Still another said: "He is at least in his 50s. It could be him."

At that moment, the front door blew open and a wind rushed in and overtook the heat of the roaring blaze in the fireplace. All of the men turned to see Ezekiel standing there, signs of the avenging angel evident yet again in his countenance. The darkness of the night and pouring rain framed this black and terrible man.

He spoke in a deep and fearsome voice and strode into the room to confront the group of men; he spoke of treachery and speaking behind one's back.

Ransom finally told him: "We think you were a Pink."

Ezekiel leveled his eyes at the man, and the speaker seemed to shrink within himself.

Another said: "Show him the book!"

The volume you, the reader, now hold in your hand, was placed in his hands, and read for the first time that night in front of that fireplace. I watched with rapt attention as the house shivered under the assault of the storm while violent lightning streaked the skies and lit up the parlor with strange and eerie flashes. Ezekiel sat, aware of all, yet absorbed by the story.

Then Cassie let out a short cry during a fearsome roll of thunder, and he sprung from his chair, only to see me frozen on the stairs. He had dismissed the men to read, and they retreated with embarrassment and deference an hour before midnight. He moved up the stairs past me, stopping to smile softly at me, and went on to check on his niece.

Her cries subsided, and I walked past her open door to see him on the side of the bed, covering her brow with his hand, softly singing. He spoke but did not look over at me.

"Sara, you should be asleep."

With that, I eased down the hallway and into bed.

As Cassie recuperated with the aid of my father's physician, I became Ezekiel's assistant, along with my brother, Samuel. We spent hours at the nearby Michigan College of Mines, pouring over mining documents and maps of the region, looking for any clues that filled in the gaps left by this journal's first entries. Ezekiel proved to be a learned man and was able to interpret many documents and financial items. As Cassie grew stronger, she was able to go riding with us.

I learned to my devastation during some of these long rides that Cassie's father had died at the same time she and her sister were taken — that he had been beaten and suffered a heart attack trying to dig through the charred wreckage of their home. He had been found a day later by her uncle, who buried him and took his name. It was no wonder why my father's inquiries into service records in Washington, D.C. had come to no fruition.

I came to know this dark stranger well, and Samuel and I accompanied him on many trips south from Houghton by rail and horse, searching for clues as related in this book. He never did admit to being a Pinkerton agent, but I was to gather his interest was professional in nature. The treasure was far secondary in our reconnaissance.

We interviewed many individuals through many towns in the area: Ewen, Watersmeet, Bruce's Crossing, Rockland, Ontonagon, Nisula, Mass City, Belt, Alston, Pelkie, Baraga, L'Anse, Tapiola, and many others. We searched newspapers, and I still recall the day we found a small obituary in the archives of the Daily Mining Gazette for a man named Henry H. Laird. I still recall Ezekiel stiffening and I saw the same fires smolder in his eyes. He asked me to copy the obituary onto a piece of paper, which I affix hereunto.

Henry was found mysteriously dead in the wilderness south of Houghton and north of Baraga at 47 years old. I can only surmise that Eli/Zeke knew him or knew of him. It was following this revelation that our searching became more intense. Zeke started going on long rides and walks in this wilderness. Here, Zeke appeared to be investigating, and his methods, to my untrained eye, appeared to be methodical and deliberate. This was no treasure hunt to him. I studied him many times: this dark, lean, and brooding individual with a hawk-like countenance that warmed only when he looked at Cassie, whose color was coming back but was still haunted by her captivity.

She and I cannot yet talk of our days there, but perhaps in time. One night, I heard tapping coming from her bedroom, and I responded. My eyes flooded with tears in memory of this sole contact in our misery. How great now are our blessings! And how great I hoped the recovery would be for this fragile girl. Zeke's eyes would warm slightly when talking to me, and I could see his concern.

One night, he asked if I would forgive him for what he did to the men found at the shack. We had found that nothing was reported of the incident, each man was recorded on township records as having died accidently, at different times during the year . . . one by suicide, found hanging in a barn in Alston;

one by logging accident; and another from a fall. Whatever suspicions the populace had, they were subverted, and the men were buried in unmarked graves.

I had responded that they deserved it, and a trial and imprisonment was too good for hateful men like that. I had bit my lip to keep from weeping and looked down at the floor. Zeke had stood and placed a hand on my shoulder. I pressed my head to his chest and cried uncontrollably. Embarrassed, I left hurriedly.

As days grew shorter and the chill of fall was in the air, Zeke was gone more and more, but would return often to check on Cassie. She was still weak, and I had resolved to mask some of my own weakness, recognizing her need as greater than mine. My mother and sister had died during childbirth, so perhaps I saw in her my lost sibling who I also had a chance to help.

One night, Zeke returned visibly weighted, and I saw clay on his boots, along with a noticeable darkening of his countenance.

Engrossed in the words before me, I snapped out of the reading to scan the forest around the mountain. I could feel something in the words I was reading, and the tiles in my mind were again slowly shivering, anxious to lock into positions. There were only a few pages to go, and I could sense the growing wonderment by my female partner. She spoke quietly.

"I think she fell in love with her rescuer."

"That isn't really that uncommon," I said.

"But the age different was significant according to what we are both seeing."

"If I were to guess, he felt something too, but I sense a streak of nobility in him and a respect for the hurt she had suffered."

I was evaluating this trail of murder and treasure like a damned romance. It was time to finish this narrative and get on with our search. If only a clue would appear. Something was floating in the back of my head, and my senses were alert as we read on. My mouth was dry, and I reached for her water bottle and Bella snatched it away.

"I don't know what diseases you may have picked up wandering around the wilderness."

"Running for my life, you mean."

"Whatever."

She punched me in the arm. What were we, 12? More eyerolling and our narrative continued as we read.

Chapter 33

"Conn, what are you hoping we would find here?" Bella asked. "To me, 150-year old clues would seem to be hard to come by."

"Mainly I am just searching for support of my theory that our mystery man came through here." I kept running into the old legend of the spirit guarding this mountain. Could this rumor have started because of our mystery man explosion that buried the entrance? Even with the diversions elsewhere, surely his pursuers would have excavated the rockslide and found the wagon if it's true. The diary mentioned he planted a few charges in the area, and I couldn't discount that he might have found a cave along the Sturgeon River gorge along the trail.

"I am thinking there's a remote possibility that these wagons were carrying bullion, either gold or silver," I said aloud. "But if our man had a wagon full of treasure, how did he conceal it from the rest of the 2,000-plus troopers, and how did his men get them disassembled and onto the Alice Dean steamboat to cross the Ohio? The question I keep asking myself is two-fold: what was the purpose of the bullion, and where was it headed?"

"Don't forget the interlaced problem," Bella interjected. "Why are we being hunted about this, what is worth killing over? Why not just go find the treasure?"

"Whoever is after us now could have had their forebears find some of what went into the river with the first wagon, and it could be the foundation of some present-day enterprise."

"That's a good point," she said. "I don't think too many people want it known that their family fortune comes from Confederate loot." She stood up and stretched, both hands extended to the sky as if reaching for something. I guess we were.

I stood as well, cutting my eyes over to our south again. "Did you hear anything? "

"No, but let's walk a bit."

As we walked, I gave her a rough sketch of Henry Laird's portion of the story.

Was Henry Laird on the trail of this treasure and the secrets associated with it? I got a slight chill when I pondered the fact that he most likely was murdered in the wilderness north of here, most likely on the same spoor that we were currently following.

My eyes shuttered momentarily.

We both froze as we heard a crack ahead of us in the underbrush, followed by soft footfalls. We both glanced at each other, silently moving east and towards the west slope of the mountain. We reached a small outcropping of stone and crouched there, weapons out.

I whispered. "We could head for higher ground for visibility, but I don't want to get surrounded up there and unable to get to the car." I put a finger to my lips, and we crouched to watch three young female hikers walk past us, 500 feet or so away, heading away from the mountain.

"Any chance your rocket-launching friends are shadowing us?" Bella slid her eyes to me.

I responded quietly. "They aren't too far away. I do have a tracker on for them to follow."

She stared at me. Another raised eyebrow softened by a touch of admiration. Maybe I imagined the admiration part.

I was also casting glances at the sky, still on the lookout for choppers. Bella glanced up as well, and we both seemed to have the same thought. We started climbing, following a path that led us higher along the south face of the mountain. Scrubby brush clung to the rocky ground, stunted pine were splashes of green, and yellow lichens spread out over the granite surfaced floor of the trail. I tapped her shoulder and indicated we would keep climbing up the trail. She nodded.

Rumors of "black helicopters" and mysterious over flights in the area had haunted the region for decades, especially out of the wilderness we were now in. I remembered reading one conspiracy theory about a white supremacist organization who supposedly had a compound in the Sturgeon or Ontonagon River gorge areas. Small, unmarked jets sometimes made appearances in the early morning and evening skies that lead to more speculation.

I was a bit dizzy with the climb. My endurance was poor, to say the least, after the events of the past week. I waved for Bella to stop, and we rested for a moment, perched on a bench of rock, and gazed out southward. With only a few leaves clinging to the trees, we were treated to a vast panorama of denuded forest — a grey ocean flecked with copper and golden fleece. Forms and undulations took shape under our glance, and I was making out vague terrain impressions through the Sturgeon Gorge wilderness spread out before us.

I closed my eyes and thought through the diary's narrative: the river crossing, the logging road, the cave, the mass of earth, the river trail, a chalky outcropping, and ultimately ending up at the mission in Keweenaw Bay. After I regained my strength, we stood, and began the descent down.

I paused to catch my breath after we crested the trail, moving across a few crags and ridges to a smooth expanse of stone. I scanned the view, picking up Limestone Mountain in the distance, wondering if that might be the 'chalky' face our mystery man took on his route.

I knew Henry Laird was part of the key. His actions dictated the route in my mind. I wasn't aware of a historic trail that came here from South Laird Road, but there was the old stagecoach route from Baraga, that ran roughly along present-day M-38, then southward along what is now Forest Highway 16. Unencumbered by the wagon, the soldier could have wandered a good deal, and indeed followed a branch of the Silver River up the Otter River, and then swing around behind

Limestone Mountain. I cast my gaze along the horizon spread in front of me and could pick out a possible route.

Stories, legends, trails, and treasure. I was beginning to think that the man's saddlebags contained some of the Mexican coins. In my imagination, which could run rampant at times, I envisioned multiple treasures — some lost with the first wagon and driver, some in the second, and lastly, in the saddlebags. Our mystery man did have a few coins in his possession at the end of his life, so there could be as many as three caches of treasure stashed in the few thousand square acres surrounding us. I believed that one had been found and was the illicit capital that spawned the demons stalking us now.

I thought back also to my own life's threads woven into this narrative. I had hit upon something when questioning the mystery of Henry Laird's life. If he had been a Pinkerton agent on the trail of Confederate loot, even 20 years after the war, it must have had significance. I thought too of the life of Joseph Alston and his railroad venture, along with the corundum and kaolin clay deposits. Both proved to be false claims, but were these cover stories for his search also for the treasure? Joseph had spent time in the mid to late 1800s in Chicago, working as a surveyor. I recalled that a Confederate agent named Thomas Hines took part in an attempted plot in 1864 to carry the war to the north with arson, the storming of confederate prisons, and the sabotage of the Union war effort in the Northwest Conspiracy.

Thomas Hines was also on General John Hunt Morgan's Great Raid that ostensibly was the origin of the wagons and men whose trail I now sought. I thought of the silver bullion. Was it destined for the hands of Confederate agents in Upper Michigan or Canada, possibly to aid in the disruption of shipping on the Great Lakes or copper mining in the Keweenaw? Now that was something to consider . . .

Historians had pontificated, postulated, and argued about the reasoning and effectiveness of Morgan's Raid ever since he was captured in July of 1863, having led Union troops on a lengthy chase throughout southeastern Ohio. Thomas Hines had also conducted "Hine's Raid" immediately prior to Morgan's Raid, with the conjectured purpose of scouting the Raid route for Morgan and obtaining horses in Indiana. He left with nearly 42 men and escaped with only himself and two others to meet Morgan at Brandenburg, right before crossing the Ohio.

What if Morgan's Raid itself was an elaborate attempt at diversion — to get the wagons and treasure escorted as far north as possible, then conduct the diversionary escape east across Indian and Ohio? Morgan spent most of the chase devising ruses and diverting detachments of troops, threatening larger cities, and generally focusing the coordinated efforts of 100,000-plus troops and militia and those of Ambrose Burnside.

While considered a failure by some, as Morgan and most of his men were captured in the end, Morgan's Raid did however raise Southern morale. In fact, Morgan would escape from his prison cell later in 1863 in Columbus, Ohio with six other men, including Thomas Hines.

Thomas Hines and Morgan would board a train near the prison and buy tickets to Cincinnati. Following a harrowing escape route through Kentucky, with Northern forces mobilized to again capture the Confederate raider, Morgan ultimately made a clean escape, largely due to Hine's efforts: Hines let himself be captured en route in Kentucky, allowing Morgan time to escape. Hines effected his escape from his captors shortly thereafter. He would go on to become one of the leading Confederate secret agents, coordinating the Southern effort in pursuit of impacting the North. Operating primarily in Canada, Hines spent time in Michigan and other Great Lakes states as well.

What if he had been involved with Confederate efforts regarding Northern operations far before 1864, and helped devise the Great Raid? It would certainly be an elaborate one, but it answered a lot of questions in my mind, or at least offered an explanation for the many racing thoughts. The possibility that the key to a Southern victory in the Civil War lay within grasp right here in Laird Township was staggering to contemplate. What form that possibly had, I didn't know.

In addition to the efforts of Pinkerton, I remembered the efforts of Lafayette Baker, who was a Michigan man, who succeeded Allan Pinkerton in 1862 as the head of the Federal Detective Police and headed up Union intelligence and counter-intelligence services. He too was directly involved in the uncovering of the Northwest Conspiracy plot. He had coined the motto "Death to Traitors" and employed hundreds of agents, usually unknown to one another. They had infiltrated the South, as Southern spies likewise infiltrated the North. He also uncovered attempts by Northern companies to trade with the South, which was of course considered a treasonous act.

Which thread from this distant past had become intertwined with my own thin thread of life? Where did that intersection occur? Did it start with my research? Simon's nocturnal visit? This diary? How did these fragments piece together? The ghosts of these individuals and their legacies walked with me on that exposed rock outcropping. I turned to each of them with questions, only to have them dissolve and fade in the mists of the timeless mystery encompassing the quest.

Bella was taking in the view. "This is amazing," she said. "I have never been up here."

"I have heard that you can see 100,000 acres from up here, half of two counties."

"I believe it. I didn't think this small of a rise would have this kind of impact."

"Just think of the view 75 years ago."

"I guess so. So what now, Sherlock?"

"I would say 'elementary' my dear, but then you would punch me, roll your eyes, cast dismissive glances my way, and generally make our partnership uncomfortable," I said.

She still rolled her eyes. ". . . But . . .?"

"I also need a ride, your intelligence, insight, and all-around generally agreeable presence."

She didn't roll her eyes this time, but it was clear she wanted to. "So where from here? Back down to look for a blasted-shut cave?"

"In a minute," I said. "I want to take this view completely. I have been keeping company with creek and river bottoms for a while now."

A moment passed and I cleared my throat. "How about you, Bella? I don't know much about you. Were you ever married?"

She looked away, looking suddenly very uncomfortable. I heard a small "Yes. Was. Eight years."

"I am sorry," I said. "So you are now . . . what . . . 27?"

She smiled. "Thank you, but add ten years to that. No need to be sorry, it didn't work out. He wanted to be somewhere with a nightlife and what he termed 'culture.' And as it turned out, he wanted to do that without me. End of story."

She paused for a moment, a far off look in her eyes before she shook her head and turned back around. "I think we need a nice quiet hike through the wilderness." She made her way over to the steeper path down the east face, calling over her shoulder: "If my vehicle is blown up, shot, or exploded, you owe me."

"Three things, Bella: blown up and exploded are the same things. Two, if we don't have a vehicle due to an unfortunate incident, we have other problems besides insurance deductibles. Three, I already owe you." She just threw up her hands ahead of me and gazed skyward without turning around. I swear I heard the words "give me strength" float up the hill to me.

I could have been imaging that too.

Chapter 34

We were greeted in the parking lot by two individuals of questionable character. Bella unslung her rifle and glanced back at me. I held up a hand and waved her firearm down. I stepped ahead, taking my place between these ruffians and my new partner. I shook both of their hands and stood back to introduce them to Bella.

"Bella, these two misanthropes are Caleb Webster and Eugene Harkness."

Caleb stepped forward first, half-bowed in a remotely gallant manner, and took her hand in his massive fist. The six-foot-two Nordic beast was built like a linebacker. He calmly reached up a hand to frame a grey-ish blond goatee and appraise her. He swiveled his head to take me into the frame as well.

"Well, I am glad there are others engaged in saving your ass besides us," he said.

"On a regular basis." This was from Gene, a compact and swarthy pirate, speaking with a wide grin from beneath a once-black mustache which was now heavy with grey.

Now it was me rolling my eyes. I started to protest, but Cal raised a hand. "Please, Conn, it will do you no good to protest. There is just a select few that can put up with you, and we are pleased to meet another tolerant and capable individual."

Gene stepped forward also, taking Bella's hand and saying: "Shake the hand of the man who shook the hand of the Lord."

Oh please.

"Gene, I don't think waving a weapon around while fishing on Prickett Dam qualifies for shaking the hand of the Good Lord, idle in your repose."

Bella interrupted. "You were the rocket launcher operator?"

Gene put on an injured expression. "What rocket launcher? I threw a rock at a seagull, and something went 'boom.' Scary stuff — dangerous places, these Upper Michigan fishing holes."

Now Bella turned to me. "I see where some of your BS comes from."

Caleb interjected. "People spend too much time in the wilderness, they start seeing and hearing things. Ma'am, have you recently been in the hospital? Hit your head? Forced to listen to roommates spouting conspiracy theories about helicopters and bad guys?" He folded his arms with great gravity, slowly shaking his head.

Bella gazed heavenward again. "I give up".

Both men chuckled, and Caleb swept a hand towards the waiting vehicles. "Shall we escort this fragile excuse for a healthy red-blooded male to his next destination?"

I pushed past him. "Thanks, Vanna, I'll take two vowels. Both an 'A.'"

Soto voce, Gene turned to Bella. "Some guys get all sensitive after four or five attempted murders. Tsk."

She finally cracked and laughed.

I turned to her. "We should look around for a couple more guys to go with these two, and then we will have complete police suspect lineup." I heard snorts of exaggerated derision behind me.

Gene banged a palm on the hood of the black Chevy crew-cab pickup parked there. "I have a few more rocks in the backseat in case we see any more seagulls." He hopped into the driver's seat while Caleb folded into the passenger seat. Rolling down the window, he winked at Bella. "I heard rabid beavers are a problem in this area, too. Don't worry; we know how to handle those hydrophobic wood choppers."

As I opened the door to Bella's car, I heard Gene yell. "20 points for use of the word hydrophobic!"

I climbed into the cab and leaned back and sighed. Bella climbed into the driver seat. "I like them," she said. "They don't put up with you either."

I murmured quietly.

"What's that, I didn't hear you?"

"I said hydrophobic is only worth five points."

She smiled and threw the jeep into reverse, rolling out in a cloud of dust. We could hear shouts of protest as the trailing vehicle pulled in behind us.

"I would like to head out to the Otter River," I said. I pulled out a map and pointed to a sharp bend in the waterway. "We knew Ezekiel must have scouted the length and breadth of the Otter River. But he didn't have a metal detector."

"Why the Otter River?" Arched eyebrow, again. Damn. That was starting to get to me.

"Because Henry Laird was found dead on the banks of the Otter northeast of here, near a camp. I think he was murdered trying to investigate and scout a burial spot for the treasure."

"How long was he in Laird Township?"

"That to me is the key. He was only here while supervisor from 1887 to 1891, and he only homesteaded from 1889 to 1891, with very little to show for it. I think he ran for supervisor as cover for searching for the treasure, wanting no property ownership problems if it was found. Something must have told him he was in the wrong area, because he packed up and moved to Baraga, apparently following another lead. I am also guessing that he ran into someone that recognized him. There were a number of Civil War veterans in the area.

"What about James Kyle?" Bella asked.

"I think he was recruited by the Pinkertons to watch Henry Laird, or perhaps Henry enlisted him in the effort. Remember, agents didn't often know one another. But they had to be friends at some point; they were buried in practically the same grave."

I snapped my fingers. Kyle. Yes.

"Simon's last name was Kyle!" I exclaimed. "I think there was his connection. He showed me a silver coin the night he was killed and said it was at the heart of a story. I think James was his great-grandfather, or some relative at the least. I am guessing there have been a few factions keeping an eye on one another for 100-plus years."

"Who gave you the diary?"

"Susan, the woman killed at her cottage in Alston, along the West Branch of the Sturgeon River."

Her eyes widened. I hadn't told her that. She shook her head wistfully. "I wish you had told me that. I should have assumed when I heard the report on the scanner."

"She was shot by a sniper, bullet intended for me."

She glanced over sharply. "Your friends weren't kidding about the murder attempts."

"You got that part right."

"Simon was Susan's brother."

I was taken aback. "How did you know them?"

"My father grew up with them."

Now it was my turn to be astonished.

"I am helping you because of them," she continued.

"Just them?"

She smiled softly, with another trace of wistfulness. "Maybe not just them."

Chapter 35

"Turn up here."

We were on a northbound dirt road, heading to a landing on the Otter River. I wanted a feel for the terrain and the chance put more pieces together. I didn't really expect to find any 150 year-old clues, especially since a century of searching had potentially revealed nothing.

We pulled up on a grassy glen next to the river, and the guys pulled up behind.

"Enjoyed eating your dust, commander," Caleb said. "Ever heard of a bathroom break? Is there a McDonalds around here?"

It never ended with those two. I wanted to finish the diary, and Bella wanted to complete the narrative as well. We kicked the doors open and read.

"Are we going to sit around reading stories?" I glanced up at Caleb; the blond bear was leaning in, a hand on the door and one on the roof of the Jeep. He was smiling his lopsided grin.

"The McDonalds is right around the corner, why don't you guys wander over that way and get something to eat?" That got me a jab in the shoulder. Bella and I moved out into the sunshine and leaned over the hood with the book, picking up where we left off:

I asked Ezekiel what had happened, and he just shook his head and excused himself, going back outside. I placed a hand on his arm outside on the porch, and he looked at me with pained eyes and said he had found where Henry Laird had been killed, or at least the last place he was known to be. He had found a hat with the initials HL along the Otter River, near the bend at the base of the bluff noted earlier in this diary. Ezekiel believed Henry had been looking for the saddlebags and someone followed him and took his life. He did manage to find one of the two men that had found the body, fashioned a raft, and floated it down the Otter. One was named Stocko Scrantany and the other was a man by the name of Fisher. Scrantany said Laird had been found with no knapsacks, or saddlebags, just the clothes on his back. They felt he had been in the woods at least a week.

Zeke had been to the L'Anse Evergreen Cemetery, and examined the gravesite of Henry, and had been vaguely disturbed that it appeared the body of his former neighbor in Laird Township was buried right next to him, a man by the name of James Kyle."

He indicated he was going to find James Kyle's family, if there was any. His disquiet came from the fact that he had known Henry some years previously, from a place he didn't want to talk about. "Maybe I will tell you someday," he told me. I don't think he will ever share, but it was some terrible place or situation, and to me it was obvious that he thought highly of Henry or that a good turn had been done by him."

The bend I wanted to investigate, and I thought was referenced in the diary, was a half-mile up-stream. We hiked up along the south side of the river and gradually swept our way north along the curve before hitting the bend. I knew there was little chance there would be any remnants of a lightning-struck tree after all these years, but I wanted the feel of the route, knowing the soldier was desperate to hide the saddlebags. In fact, I wasn't even sure if the saddlebags had been found.

"Again, I apologize for the obvious question, but what are we looking for?" Bella was again skeptical.

"Ye of little faith," I said. "I have no idea. Well, any concrete ideas."

Gene volunteered. "You gave us a rough lay of things over the phone, and now we are looking for a third part of the treasure?"

We walked around the curve of the bend with small maple saplings whipping at our legs; the ground was soft and pungent along the river.

I stopped and visually followed the remainder of the curve through the forest cover. Damn. The only thing resembling a bluff was at least 500 feet away. I may have had the wrong spot. Catching the eyes of my compatriots, our motley band tromped over to the base of the bluff. I had paced it at 600 feet.

Too far . . . except . . . here. Winding away to the right along the bluff was a hollowed-out wash.

"The diary indicated a curve along a bluff," I said. "I think the river wound along here when it was at a higher stage and before this young stream found another path. A lot can happen in over 150 years. Let's climb it."

We scrambled up a narrow fissure in the face, sliding in the clay soil. We crested at the top of what proved to be about a 30-foot embankment. Sun caught glistening drops of the heavy fall dew in the open glen in front of us. The shape of the meadow was ovoid, with the narrow point at the eastern portion.

"I bet we find a logging road up there," I said. "The map shows a few dotted lines through the area."

Gene and Caleb glanced at each other and shrugged. "So where is the treasure?" Gene asked.

"I am convinced our friend from 1863 passed through here. The Keweenaw Bay Mission is east by northeast roughly six miles from here. It is entirely possible he took the wagon through the Silver Mountain area, buried it, and then traveled through here. He may have considered heading northeast along what is now M-26, and continued along the military road, but that would have been an obvious route of his pursuers."

I walked over to the edge of the bluff and peered over, spotting a massive, uprooted stump halfway down the slope, with the rotting remains melting into the forest floor beyond.

"It wouldn't take long to convince me that this was the tree under which he buried the saddlebags," I said. "The erosion over the years has taken away what was left of its foundation."

I pointed out in front of me; the tree had fallen almost due west from its position.

Bella clamped a pair of headphones on and jumped over the bank, sliding down the slick slope and balancing the metal detector in front of her much like a high-wire performer might navigate his narrow path. She was getting into the whole Caleb and Gene vibe. That wasn't a good thing. Gene clapped me on the back and followed her down the slope. Caleb and I exchanged a glance, and retraced our ascent route back to the bottom. Bella was expertly scanning the area.

She stopped after about 10 minutes and pointed. Gene lifted his shovel and drove it at the spot directed, and lifted the loamy earth, sifting it slightly and then dumping it. Bella scanned and nodded. Gene struck again and followed the same procedure. Bella swept her instrument like a mine detector, smiled, and dropped a gloved hand into the dirt, half concealed from my vantage point.

"What is it?" I half-dared not ask.

She reached back and twisted her body away from me, a half-smile forming at the corners of her lips. A gleam of triumph flashed briefly. "Nothing," she said.

I held out my hand anyway. She dropped a dirt-encrusted round metal object into my hand.

We had work to do.

Chapter 36

Three hours later, we were back at the vehicles with Gene's tailgate open, looking at a small fortune in coins of varying size. There were also the rotting remains of what once had been saddlebags, with brass buckles still clinging to the remnants of the leather. I had rubbed a few clean. Some of the smaller were gold coins, and I could make out what appeared to be Spanish lettering. The larger coins were identical to the one Simon gave me on that rainy evening that seemed a lifetime ago. It almost was a few lifetimes ago for me, truly.

We covered up our excavation with leave and I hoped it would soon snow, or our mystery might come to a conclusion.

"Were there really two wagon loads of these coins?" Caleb looked skeptical.

"I don't think so," I responded. "There may have been some, but I believe there was something else of importance"

"Where to next?" Gene asked. "We are getting hungry. From here, we can run to town if you two will stay out of trouble for the briefest of moments?"

I turned to Bella. "See what having friends like this does! Found a lost treasure, people trying to kill us, century-old mysteries, and they worry about their food."

Caleb managed to look injured.

"I think your friends are trying to give us a moment to figure out our next move and cover the rest of the diary, Einstein."

I rolled my eyes. We opened Bella's rear Jeep door and arrayed our weaponry while Gene and Caleb drove off.

"You certainly know how to show a girl a good time, Conn." Her cheeks were touched with red; we had most surely had an interesting day thus far.

We loaded up our loot, took our rifles into the cab, and again opened the diary again:

My father and I went to the Houghton County Courthouse and visited with a Mr. Nichols who served as a law enforcement representative for the Laird Township area. I had given them the descriptions of some of the men that came to . . . visit me while I was imprisoned. I only had a few names, and we had little to go on. He dryly mentioned that Zeke had made a return visit to the sawmill and was informed that a handful of men had quit and left the area. His methods of dealing with my captors had proved an effective house-cleaning method.

Ezekiel had also made contact with James Kyle's son, Thomas. Thomas indicated that his father and Henry had been friends. Ezekiel had made inquiries into local records and found that James had never been married, that Thomas was an illegitimate child whose mother had died, and that Thomas lived in his father's old cabin on a road near the settlement of

Nisula. Thomas worked odd jobs for local farmers, helping with haying season and such matters. He had the social stigma that some referred to in most unkind terms, which I shall not relate here. Ezekiel confided to me that he felt Thomas played up that role and kept to the fringes of what passed for society, possibly hiding a deep intelligence and knowledge. Thomas would not relent, and steadfastly refused to admit any knowledge of what Henry and his father discussed at any meetings.

Ezekiel also searched Houghton county records at the courthouse, looking for land and property deeds. He felt most strongly that Henry had instigated the formation of the township and offered services as supervisor to provide cover for his investigations in the area. No other reason made sense, he said. His short time as a property owner most likely served two purposes. One was to appear to be a legitimate landowner in the township named for him, the homestead sealing his position and status. The second was possibly he had uncovered clues on the property relating to the location of some of the treasure. Being township supervisor also allowed him to traverse the length and breadth of the township unfettered, and he could visit locals and engage their knowledge of events long passed.

The Silver Mountain legend intrigued Ezekiel, as he believed some of the treasure was silver, but he found old hand-drawn maps that indicated old designations in the area as "Silver" prior to the Civil War. Still, Zeke was undeterred.

Bella, who was leaning into me again, wondered out loud. "I bet Simon Kyle is a great-grandson of James."

I was thinking the same thing. But seeing where he lived, I could only assume he never found the treasure. We read on, but I had a feeling we were about to find out in the diary that Ezekiel had given the coin to young Thomas Kyle. That made the most sense. Simon had also said "we" were watching, referring to his evaluation of me. There was Susan, the woman that gave me the diary, entrusting a gift to me that had cost her life. Were there other players in this drama as well?

So many bodies — Simon, Susan, Davey and Zack, Josh, possibly Eunice and Yancy, and almost me numerous times. Not to mention Henry Laird, possibly the young Confederate soldiers, Thomas McGhee, and who knows how many others? I had vengeance on my mind of course, but it was becoming muted as the mystery deepened. Finding this portion of whatever treasure existed had but whet my appetite to figure out the rest of the mystery, and ultimately find information to stop whoever was hunting us. And by stopping them, I knew it might mean more death, and I hoped it wasn't mine.

Chapter 37

I looked up from the diary on the center console of the vehicle and looked around. It has been said that when facing death, details come into focus much more clearly, especially the small and beautiful things that had gone unnoticed during one's lifetime. It was most certainly true. While the past few days had been a blur, it was the interludes that arrested me internally when I looked around: the splashes of muted reds, the gold of fallen poplar leaves, the stark contrast of balsam and pine green against the grey of the surrounding maples and oaks. From somewhere far distant, we caught a wisp of cedar smoke, its sweet tang almost joyful in the gathering coolness. Fall was indeed beautiful deep in the woods here in the western Upper Peninsula, but now death moved in the beauty, and foreboding skies hovered just out of our reach.

I flexed my fingers, which had stiffened in the digging operation. I gazed down. Did these fingers, which turned back the pages of history, inadvertently summon the death-angel of forgotten secrets? The backs of my hands were crisscrossed with scars and scratches, emblematic of the years of my life. I certainly had a background to deal with some of the recent events and was grateful for the tools given to me. I was most grateful for the acquaintance of two good men, and now Bella.

I prayed these hands would yet guide me, carrying me through the fiery trials I knew we had yet to face. Let the angel come.

A blue jay had taken to a branch in a small red pine just off the front of the car and was calling, "Thief, thief," which was possibly an apt approbation to some extent. I elbowed Bella and said, "He is talking to you."

She was learning. She just ignored me.

A ground mist was forming a physical curtain around the small glade we were in, and I felt an oppressive sense in the lack of sightlines away from the vehicle. I turned the engine on, and a blast of warm air greeted the windshield, attempting to clear it.

I cracked a window, and Bella and I looked wordlessly at each other, the question on both of our minds: how long do we wait here? I answered by throwing the diary up on the dash, putting the vehicle in drive, spinning our way out of the clearing, and heading for the safety and comfort of the myriad of wooded roads in northern Laird Township. Bella had a handgun in her lap, and one of the rifles was pointed muzzle-first into the footwell on her side of the car, the stock close at hand between us.

I gave her Gene's cell number, and she tried calling him, but didn't get a signal.

"Keep trying. I will keep moving south. We should be fine once we get around Limestone Mountain" I was referring to the other prominent rise of land in Laird Township, two miles north by northwest of Alston. I wanted to take a quick stop on the south side, where some quarrying had resumed after a few years of inactivity. Bella gave me a sharp glance as we pulled up to a gate along the south side.

I pointed through the windshield at the face of the quarried side of the mountain, the yellow-white of the exposed limestone shone in the lingering light of the day.

"I could easily see our friend coming through here," I said. "He mentioned a chalky bluff."

I took out the Forest Service map and unfolded it on our laps. I pointed to Silver Mountain and traced my finger up the page to where we were at Limestone Mountain. Continuing nearly straight up the page, it took us to the bend in the Otter River where we found the coins.

"This route makes sense according to the diary," I continued. "But I still would like to see some aerial photographs of the Sturgeon River Valley. Joseph Alston had claimed he had found a wall of white clay for making porcelain along that valley. So that wouldn't be 'chalky,' but maybe portions of it are. The key for me would be the fact he was moving away to the northeast when he left what we think is the Silver Mountain area. He had also indicated that after burying the saddlebags, he made his way to the mission, which I still assume was on Keweenaw Bay, nearly due east from where he buried the coins we just found."

"But he indicated that he placed charges only and blew the face to decoy his pursuers."

Indeed, according to his own words, there should be nothing there. I just wanted to confirm a thought process. Working back from the saddlebags and retracing his route places him closer to Silver Mountain than Ontonagon, so I think we were in the general area."

I continued. "I have also been thinking of the Indian legend of the guardian of Silver Mountain. Perhaps the legend originated from someone hearing the original explosion. Or maybe our friend planted additional charges that someone ran into. Hard to say. I think it is worth more investigation."

I pulled back out onto North Laird Road and followed it westward to a long hill and a four-cornered intersection with an incredible view of southern Houghton County. We pulled off at the intersection. Bella she got out and looked around, astonished at the panoramic sweep of thousands of acres spread out south and east from what locals called North Laird Heights.

"This is incredible, Conn. All these years, I never drove up here."

I smiled and nodded. "This has always been a favorite spot of mine. I first proposed up here . . . " My voice trailed off. It was pretty painful to think about now.

She looked over at me standing there, her eyes glistening a bit too. "Conn, there are places that are difficult for me, also, but we should be grateful we have a place to remember, along with a moment strong enough to linger after all these years."

I looked down at the ground, then up at the sky, taking in the graceful sweep of a magnificent expanse of sky. "I am indeed fortunate to have places like this to remember. Songs do that for me, too, taking me back to a place and time forever etched on the tapestry of history."

"Are you a poet, too, Conn?" Her smile was gracious and warm, the tone gently teasing. I gave her an embarrassed look and shrugged. "Everyone needs a place of beauty to go to, either inside or external."

It was her turn to give me an embarrassed look. "Your friends gave me a brief snapshot of your time with them. They indicated that you had done something pretty amazing and got badly hurt doing it."

I said nothing as she gently continued. "Thank you, for the sake of all those women. They said there were a dozen women saved in that fire." She paused as my eyes narrowed. In memory. In some silent, unspeakable pain.

I said quietly, "But four died in that fire. That still haunts me."

"But you got the guys that set the fire, Conn, and saved so many. Gene said you went back into that inferno over a dozen times, carrying women out who had collapsed in the smoke."

"They were right there with me. They were incredible. I am still haunted by those who we couldn't reach." I stared out the window, lost in that moment of memory and flames.

She reached over to me, put her hand on my shoulder, and spoke softly. "Evil men imprisoned those women, and set that fire to cover their escape. You did all you could, I hope you know that."

As she spoke, she reached out for a half-hug, our shoulders bumping, when her cell phone buzzed.

"The cavalry is on campaign again," I said before answering "Where are you guys?"

I could hear Gene's voice faintly.

Bella turned questioningly to me, repeating the query with her eyes.

"Can we all meet at your house?" I asked her. "I want to see my dog. Then we will go visit Marge."

She nodded and relayed the address and directions to the guys. Bella and I cast one more glance at the far eastern horizon as a reverential hush was settling down over the vast expanse before us. The brilliant sunset behind us was casting a pink and orange glow onto the reflecting clouds before us. It was a glorious fall evening, leaving us silent in its beauty.

Damn. I was turning into a poet.

As we both reached the car, we looked at each other over the cab, catching ourselves for a moment in what could have been. Climbing in, she engaged the console shifter into drive, and, making a slow turn on the intersection, reached over and briefly squeezed my hand. The briefest of a half-imagined sighs came over to me. I felt that way too, but wondered: how did she get to drive again? Her car?

Danger had heightened our senses, making them keen and honed to the unseen vibrations of the mystery and elements lurking just out of our grasp. We could both feel the oppression of that uncertainty; it lay like a heavy, sodden wool blanket across us as we drove. I could sense a freshening breeze coming and prayed it would not be a whirlwind that would take our lives.

As undersheriff in Houghton County, Bella maintained residence here, right on the Baraga County line, halfway to

Houghton along the Tapiola Road. I had driven by her driveway many times over the years, not realizing that there was a house a quarter mile back from the road, along a narrow tree-lined, two-track road. We followed a broken wood fence for half the distance and turned into the yard of a well-kept home. It was more cabin than house, with timbering present at the entry, and evidence of a stout frame backing up the tan wood siding.

Bella pulled to a stop, and I heard excited barking coming from inside the home.

I don't believe I'd had a more joyful reunion or more moving experience in my life. Grey was more a furry, loving missile than playful dog. I hugged back with all of my might, kissing his forehead and whispering every pet name I ever had for my handsome boy. He wriggled, squirmed, licked, and mauled me into the grass.

"Okay, boy, I give up. I'm sorry — take it easy!" God how I missed him, and his departed brother. He got enough hugs for both.

Bella watched for a moment, and then gave us our time to romp for a while in the yard. She came out and told me that coffee was on. I heard a rumble of engines, and my erstwhile compatriots came roaring up the driveway.

"Spend our money yet, Conn?" Caleb yelled from the rolled-down window.

"Sure, every store around here takes Mexican silver bullion." I smiled back.

He nudged Gene, and I heard him speak loudly enough for me to hear. "He is feeling better."

Chapter 38

We sat in the yard and witnessed the remnants of the day fade, watchful in the half-light. We still had an unknown nemesis behind the attacks that had left a trail of bodies across southern Houghton County and perhaps we were on the cusp of discovering yet other long-hidden secret that had claimed the lives of countless unknown others over the last 150-plus years.

Caleb and Gene offered to stay outside, keeping eyes on the skies and surrounding property. Bella and I sat at her kitchen table and laid the dairy out in front of us, with Grey lay at my feet, a happy sigh resonating from deep within him. There were but a few pages left:

Ezekiel came to see me on a dark and windy night. He stood on the front porch in mud-spattered and blood-stained clothing. He had elicited retribution on men in nearby Ontonagon County and had freed three more girls. His face was terrible in its resolution. He had burned a place to the ground and shot who knows how many others as they tried to escape. He said it was near the Firesteel Rivers along the Copper Range Railroad. He had found the trail of yet another group that escaped to Canada, and was ready to set off again, but had come to pay his respects and to say goodbye to me. I clung to him in the blackness of night and implored him not to go. I inquired as to the resolution of the mystery of Henry Laird's death.

His voice was that of quiet resolution, and he admitted that he had known Henry in the Secret Service, the organization born out of the Union Intelligence Service during the last days of the War Between the States. He and others had been tracking former Confederate officers in Canada and the Midwest. Ezekiel had been part of the Union forces to enter Richmond, only to sift through the ashes of the records of the Confederate Secret Service, burned by agents as they withdrew. A few tattered pieces of paper alluded to an effort in 1863 to send explosives, agents, and bullion north into Michigan, with the aim of doing harm to the copper industry, the iron ore industry, and the locks at Sault Ste. Marie.

He had been employed by the federal government and allied with the Pinkertons for nearly 30 years. It was known that a number of rogue agents intended to find the lost explosives and continue to serve what was now known as The Lost Cause. Agents had travelled thousands of miles and scoured forests, rivers, fields, and towns to find the rumored treasure and various means of vengeance. Records of interviews with Confederate prisoners of John Hunt Morgan's Great Raid, who had been captured at Buffington Island and West Point, Ohio, and follow-up visits were made. Morgan had of course been killed in 1864 in Tennessee, and others, including Basil Duke and Thomas Hines, said nothing. Participants in the Raid related that the strange cavalcade of horses, buggies, a hearse, a circus wagon, and numerous other wagons had unknown fates following their ultimate capture. It was also said a number of them dropped out the Raid, and men left in the night with unknown destinations — some deserters, and others that were known to be passionately loyal to Morgan and the Cause simply disappeared.

Ezekiel, Henry, and others conjectured that the Raid had served the purpose of reconnoitering near prisoner of war camps at Camp Randall, near Madison, Wisconsin; Camp Douglas near Chicago; and Camp Morton near Indianapolis; and other military installations, but felt most strongly that the entire seemingly-wasted Confederate effort was in fact a massive diversion to move instruments of destruction far north and accomplish these nefarious ends.

But Ezekiel said that the trail had gone cold, and his mission of mercy, undertaken following his retirement from the service, to track and free young women like me, was too important to abandon. He owed it to his brother and to others who suffered as I did. I cried great tears on his shoulder, and impulsively kissed him fiercely there in the gathering blackness. He held me briefly and then moved into the house and up the stairway. I heard voices and great sobs and a plea rendered much like mine to stay. But it was for naught.

He looked upon me there in the lantern light on the porch with eyes of deep sadness, the lines even more pronounced upon his face. He asked what greater love could one man have than to free those who knew no hope, who cried for mercy, and who knew fear. I was downcast but knew in my heart and *from bitter experience that fierce and driven men were necessary to accomplish this shining goal. I was ashamed of my selfishness.*

He asked if I would look after his niece and said he would return when he could. I told him I would write of him in this book, to memorialize him, a mission, a Lost Cause, and clues to a great mystery. I only wish I could relate indeed the great mystery of my heart. And his.

Bella and I looked at each other. She brushed away tears from the corner of her eyes. She smiled. "That was beautiful," she said. "Is beautiful."

There was one last entry, dated July 11th, 1910:

I received a letter today. I cannot write its contents here; it is too painful.

There was a quick rap on the door and Gene poked his head in. "Vehicles coming up the driveway."

I put the diary in a bag and put it in Bella's freezer. She stared at me, but then moved towards the door, racking an AR-15 as she moved out onto the porch. The four of us fanned out in the yard. Grey growled deep within himself and moved out to my left, his teeth bared. Two black Suburbans ground the gravel as they turned into the driveway, and we leveled our weapons and spread out even more. Gene had the rocket launcher on his shoulder, and Caleb had moved off around the back of the house to check for flankers and cover our rear.

The doors of each vehicle swung open slowly, and an older man with a swept-back shock of white hair, a patrician air, and power stepped out and looked around. He half-held his hands out in front of him and moved out across the lawn towards us, as other men dressed in black poured out of the vehicles, taking up position near the open doors.

"That is far enough." My voice carried well at that distance.

"My, my," his voice carried an air of authority and condescension. At last, the individual who might be behind this whole nightmare. "May I come into the house? he asked. "We have much to discuss."

"Not with your army," I said. "You can do your talking right here."

A break in the voice. He grunted a command, and his men re-entered their vehicles and pulled away back down the drive. They stopped at the main highway; we could see their lights in the ground-fog, a quarter mile away.

"Satisfied?" he asked. "I am unarmed."

I waved my rifle toward the porch, and he moved past me with a brief stagger at the three steps needed to ascend her porch. He entered her foyer, followed by Caleb, who frisked him expertly, and went back out on the porch. I could hear him talking in low tones with Gene. This definitely had a feeling of anticipation, to say the least.

"May I sit?" the man asked.

I had a momentary flashback to Simon making a similar request in what seemed like ages ago. He pulled the chair to the table and steepled his fingers before him. "Constantine, you and I have had an interesting dance over the past week."

He smiled, exposing capped white teeth. I could see the faint weavings of a hairpiece at his forehead as well. I also could comment on his tan and gold chain at his throat. All these things pissed me off even more.

I sat across from him. Bella leaned against a counter. I had flashbacks also to Lauren. A dark night. A mysterious visitor.

"I think we are due to have a little exchange of information." He lifted his chin and regarded me from under heavy brows. "You also owe me for two helicopters, forcing my use of . . . ground transportation."

"Do you call a half-dozen murder attempts an 'exchange of information?' " I asked, exasperated. "Let's discuss what you owe me!"

He looked at me contemptuously. I slowly drummed the fingers of one hand on the table. I really wanted to hit him.

"Before you do anything stupid, I think you should look at this." He reached slowly into a vest pocket in his blazer and took out a smartphone. He pressed a few buttons and handed it over to me. I stared wordlessly at the screen, handed it to Bella, and clenched my hands into fists. A bright, shining, red star had fallen from the sky and exploded in my field of vision, blinding me to all. Bella gasped.

It was a clear video shot of Lauren. She was sitting on a shabby metal-framed bed. I could see dirty sheets as the cameraman pulled away to show barred windows and a door which was also heavily-barred. I mentally recoiled when I saw

Lauren mouth something wordlessly to the camera and was backhanded by a figure that moved from the left, causing her to slam back into the wall.

My words came from a bottomless pit, deep in the angry fire of this fallen sun. "Start talking."

"I am glad we understand each other."

I slammed my fist into the table, roaring to my feet and grabbing him by the front of his jacket. "You will die in the most painful way imaginable if another hair on her head is harmed."

He gave me a half-shocked wicked smile, and his forked tongue slithered out to lick his dry lips.

I punched him, and he flew back from his half-risen position, falling back against the kitchen countertop. He wiped blood from his face and stood erect. He spat, then said "You don't want to do that again."

But I did.

Bella spoke quietly in the intervening space. "Conn, we should hear what he has to say."

So I let him sit again. He composed himself and asked for a glass of water.

"You can go drown yourself in Lake Superior for all I care," she hissed. "You heard him, start talking." She showed the venom that the video engendered in her. I was proud of her for that, even though it meant whatever we had or felt for each other was impacted heavily by the revelation.

So he spoke. The words were said with an attempt at authority but rang hollow in the confines of the small kitchen.

I was curious to follow his narrative, but also aware that there would be half-truths and most likely all-out lies uttered.

"Where are you holding my wife?"

"She is safe now, pending our discussions," he said. "I was given to understand she is your ex-wife? Such concern."

"Your story."

Chapter 39

"My name is Thaddeus Wesley Moore," the man said.

I kept a straight face, displaying no emotion. I had indeed deduced that back at the Alston town hall, but I let him continue.

"You uncovered some clues and are on the trail of something very important to us. We wish for that information to be subverted and you abandon any goods, clues, or material of substance to us."

"Or . . . ?"

"I think idle threats are counterproductive. You have bore witness to the scope of my power and reach. I have access to more resources than you can imagine."

"Moore Industries," I said. "Logging, transportation, trucking, shipping, manufacturing . . . Fifth largest private company in Wisconsin and Michigan."

He corrected me. "The Midwest, actually."

Whatever, I had only done a record search on him a few days ago. It was time to play this out.

"Shouldn't it be Wesley Industries? Founded with Confederate gold and miscellaneous robberies in Michigan and Wisconsin? Your current glossy image gets kind of fuzzy when looked at with a different lens."

"Ah, we were correct. You do have something. I wouldn't cast aspersions on any company with roots 150 years old. Behind every great fortune, there is a crime."

"Thank you for the bastardization of Balzac, Thad. What is it you suspect?"

"I think you know my ancestor made a certain . . . 'acquisition' in 1863."

"If killing a Confederate soldier and fishing a fortune out of the Ontonagon River can be called acquisition, Thad."

"You can call me Mr. Moore. We were at war; a found treasure from ill-gotten Rebel gains is not robbery."

"Sorry, Thad. I think the string of murders committed by your family and company over the last 150 years makes it a relevant series of crimes. You've never found the other wagon, have you?"

"Actually, there were three. John Hunt Morgan had sent two north from Vernon, and another was hidden by Thomas Hines on his previous raid into Indiana a week earlier."

"I am guessing your mineral exploration arm has searched the Sturgeon River Valley without success for quite a while. Your helicopter with sensors and scanning equipment has been noticed for almost 20 years."

"We found the first wagon. It was loaded with coal, no treasure, no bullion. At least that is what we thought."

"But it was very special coal, wasn't it, Thad?" I asked.

Bella glanced over sharply at me.

"Indeed. My great-great grandfather and his men examined every piece in the wagon. There were a number that were very heavy. It turned out a few were actually –"

"Courtenay Torpedoes," I finished for him. As the Confederate war situation became increasingly dire, a number of explosives were fashioned to look like coal — explosives in an iron shell dipped in pitch or beeswax and covered in coal dust. Agents slipped north with them, planting them in fuel piles used in Union shipping and manufacturing. Two famous and devastating uses of them were at the both the Union supply depot in City Point, Virginia, which caused hundreds of deaths, and possibly in the sinking of the Sultana, a steamboat carrying wounded Union soldiers and former prisoners of war as the war was closing. The President of the Confederacy had outlawed the use of the torpedoes against soldiers and civilians, as he considered them cowardly.

"I had thought the coal torpedoes were not in use until 1864?" I was mildly interested.

"So did a great many people, but there they were. Perhaps Mr. Hines was testing them."

I continued with the narrative, interrupting him. "They were sending the wagons north to disrupt the copper mining Industry, the iron ore industry, and the Soo Locks."

He looked up at me shrewdly. "We were right in our assessment — you have uncovered a lot of information. Remarkable considering the men I had hunting you. But yes, the South knew that over 80% of the copper used in the production of brass in the war effort in the North. The copper used for cannons, shell casings, and the like came from the Keweenaw Peninsula. They wanted to stop it. My progenitor, shall we say . . . 'interviewed' the young men he traced to a logging camp. Young George and Isaac had no idea about the whereabouts of Thomas McGhee but were persuaded to describe the wagons and speculate on their important contents."

"The coal fished out of the spilled wagon on the Ontonagon River was just that -- coal. But the startling discovery of the splintered wagon, soon pulled from the water, was . . . inspirational."

I had guessed this, too. "The reinforced bed was filled with gold bullion."

I got sharp glances from both Thad and Bella with that one. A guess, but it had to be to justify 150 years of murder.

"John Hunt Morgan never would have embarked on his great diversion had he known about the explosives, so the third wagon that previously crossed the Ohio River into Indiana contained the explosives. The other two, that he escorted, contained the gold, or so he thought."

"And you and your rotten family haven't found the second 'gold' wagon."

Thad looked almost wistful. "I would love to have been there when they pulled apart the wagon's false bottom, splintered from the fall from the bridge into the river. It is said that there was over 2,500 pounds . . . roughly $50,000,000 in today's money."

I heard Bella draw a deep breath.

I didn't wait for a reply on that figure. "So the root of all your evil was indeed money."

"The money was legitimate war confiscation and used to create much good."

I didn't snort, but I think my viewpoint was understood. "Your evil empire, you mean. I already mentioned all the killing you did to protect the secret. Henry Laird?"

He shrugged. "Henry was a Pinkerton; he spent a few years in the area, trying to find evidence against my great-great-grandfather. He had interests in logging, so Henry had spent time in a number of mills and shipyards owned by my family. We had a large operation in Baraga, where Henry worked as a laborer, or posing as one, in the years after the war. He caused a great deal of damage to our organization as he spied on us for over a decade. His untimely end was fortuitous. My forebears felt he was close to finding the rest of the gold but could not risk further exposure of our operations."

I reached into a pocket and withdrew a coin. As Simon did, I took it and spun it on the tabletop; it twirled for ten seconds before settling in front of our unwanted guest.

He lifted a corner of his mouth, half-sneer and half-smile. "Old Henry did find something, didn't he? He didn't mention that as he died. My grandfather was there — he said nothing."

"Saddlebags filled with silver."

"Hines hadn't mentioned those—"

I interrupted again. "Is it safe to say that Wesley had been contacted by Hines and knew about the wagons? Instead of aiding the movement north, he decided to steal them? I am guessing that this rotten bastard trafficked in women and kidnapped girls, too."

"You have put a lot of this together, haven't you? Yes, Wesley had been contacted by Hines on his Raid, which was in essence a scouting expedition for the Great Raid, especially this component." He gave an impatient shrug and spoke through a half-sneer. "Women were part of the equation. I am indifferent to their role of progress and empire-building. Building takes men and financing, men need women."

I held back the rage that was building in me. I had him talking and didn't want to break his stride. He was very nearly bragging.

"And he followed the wagons north, so he could kill the teamsters and the gold?" I asked.

"Soldiers. They were soldiers. Fighting a war."

"They were renegades and thieves. Did he know about the gold, Thad?"

"No, but he suspected. It had to be important. He was to follow at a distance and cover the rear as they moved north, but . . . Enough of this. Where is the last wagon, Conn? Lauren's life and yours may depend on it."

I was back to getting pissed again. "I don't have anything. A trail of clues. A lot of attempts on my life. That's it."

He rose to his feet, his affected glacial calm cracking. He pointed a bony finger at me and jabbed. "Give me what you have, or you die today."

"So could you, but first I want you to witness your little empire come crumbling down."

227

"And just how do you figure that?"

"Well, everything today is recorded and videotaped. You have admitted to murder, and my attempted murder, and I am sure the mention of a Confederate stolen treasure will sit well with your stockholders."

He was shaking with rage. "I employ thousands of people! Are you going to threaten Standard Oil next? I tell you, every great fortune and visionary in the country got his start with something of questionable merit."

"Questionable merit, Thad? Interesting rationalization on murder."

He sat again, waving a hand. "Water! Get me water!"

Bella smiled, but it did not touch her eyes. "You already have my answer on that, Thad."

She really was spending too much time with me. Attitude, sarcasm, the whole nine yards. Good for her. I am a good role model.

"Let's go for a ride," I said.

Chapter 40

We wound down the driveway with Thad in the backseat. I sat next to Bella, hand on my gun.

Bella glanced sideways at me, probably wondering if I had lost my mind.

Thad's troop carrier pulled into the road after us, closely followed by Gene and Caleb, who were our rearguard for the trip.

I pointed ahead, and we drove south until we hit M-38 and made our way to Alston. I tapped Bella's knee, and she pulled off to the left. We got out, and I walked up to a familiar house. I told Thad to knock on the door.

A familiar woman's voice echoed from inside, and then Marge came to the door, wiping her hands on a dishtowel. She did an appropriate doubletake as she opened the door.

"Hello, Marge," I said. "I would introduce you, but I believe you know each other."

She gave all the expected disclaimers and protests, but I waved her down. Thad just looked straight ahead, ignoring both of us.

"Marge, it was too coincidental that another murder attempt occurred as I pulled out of your driveway," I said. "I am guessing you made a few calls. And you made sure to graciously lend me your car. There would be no mistaking me or what I was driving. "

I turned to Bella, sweeping an open hand towards the two on the porch. "Meet the current living progeny of the Wesley and Carlyle clans. Thick as thieves and just as dirty, over 150 years of murder, carrying on the family tradition."

The two said nothing. Glares of hatred were wasted on me. I continued. "But due to recent downturns in the industrial world, and market losses, our good friends here decided to dip their toes in the drug trade. Marge handled the local meth labs and pill dealers. Marijuana was going legal in Michigan, so they stuck with hard drugs, mixing in heroin and miscellaneous opioids."

I was speculating, but the looks on their face told me I was right.

Still nothing from our audience. Thad's men had gotten out of the trailing vehicles and were covered by Gene and Caleb who had shouldered their weapons. We heard sirens on the highway, headed our way from both east and west. Bella had made calls.

"Thad, it was important to get you on the record. Much of my theory was supposition — it was nice of you to fill in the gaps."

"You have nothing," he protested. "It is all old stories. Proof. You need proof."

"Oh, I think the search warrant will fill in a few details here in Marge's house. I also think brother and sister should spend more time together."

Law enforcement vehicles poured into the yard. Thaddeus started impassively at me, a gleam in his eye. "Aren't you forgetting something?"

"Let's see . . . murder, murder, murder, attempted murder, murder, kidnapping . . . wait, are you referring to Lauren?"

He blinked, not understanding.

"Bella got a text from authorities down in Eagle River and the Wisconsin State Police. A warrant was served on your headquarters a half-hour ago. Lauren was found locked in the basement. You had a few guards who cooperated quite nicely. Two didn't and are currently on their way to the hospital. I am kind of wondering if they have thought of possible midnight attacks in their room?" I continued. "Everyone in your office is currently under lockdown, waiting for the FBI to arrive. Computer experts are on the way too, I am sure we will find some interesting records there, too. I am guessing you can explain the safe filled with cash? Drug money is so hard to launder, Thad."

He lunged at me, his powerful body twisting out of itself. I dropped to one knee, half-turning my torso, striking upward, intersecting the arc of his hammer-blow with an uppercut palm strike to his chin. He dropped like a stone, crashing to the ground, rolling off the side of my boots. His jaw hung, shattered from his unbelieving face.

"That was for touching my wife."

Bella eyed me speculatively, "We need to talk about how you met Gene and Caleb. I don't think you learned that move in history class. "

"Yoga."

Marge spat obscenities at me, her matronly face contorted in fury. Two officers came and cuffed her, leading her to a car. We could hear her screams across the lot as the cruiser door slammed shut. I recognized Stone Face, and he walked up with a grin. He stuck his hand out.

Gee, maybe he wasn't such a bad guy.

He then surprised me and gave Bella a big hug. She looked surprised, but relief was in her face. He left to rejoin the line-up of hired help. One officer was calling for an ambulance.

"Who brought the warrant?" Bella asked.

A young female officer, smartly attired in bulletproof vest and in black combat gear, produced one from a metal clipboard and handed it to her.

"Shall we?"

Chapter 41

"You aren't supposed to be in here, Conn."

"Okay." I rolled my eyes. Bella sighed and beckoned me in. Marge had bread baking, so I turned off the oven out of courtesy and opened the door to let the heat out. "Don't touch anything else, Conn. We need evidence out of here."

I knew where I was headed. I had a suspicion. Marge had a grand bookshelf, filled with dusty volumes and tomes that appeared to be far out of the budget of a township treasurer. Indeed, looking around at leather furniture and what appeared to be expensive antiques, the interior of the home outdid the humble ranch exterior. She had lived well on drug money and a legacy of evil.

I grabbed a pair of gloves from a young male lab technician, who scowled at me from beneath an ill-fitting baseball cap. "Get a haircut, young man, high and tight," I said. "Talk to Steve, he will set you up with his barber." More scowls. I smiled at him to rob my words of any offense, and he finally grinned back.

I started pursuing the bookshelves, running a finger over the spines, until I came to an old, richly-appointed leather volume which I pulled from the shelf. The cover indicated it was a King James Bible. I knew whose it was, and indeed, this was what I had hoped to find. The inscription read:

To Henry, may God go with you. Jane

I thumbed through the pages, Bella coming up to read at my shoulder.

"Is that what I think it is?" she asked.

"Yes, this is Henry Laird's Bible, pilfered by the pious Mr. Carlyle, himself part of the conspiracy to protect the secrets Henry was here to uncover. Jane was Henry's mother."

I turned it upside down and a few papers, yellowed with age, floated out onto the wood floor. I picked them up; they were all notes for sermons or jotted notes from meetings with parishioners. I turned my attention to the covers and inserted a knife from my belt into the heavy bound leather. I wondered out loud. "Is it called 'Corinthian' leather because it is usually found on Bibles?"

Bella jabbed me with an elbow. I relented, carefully worked the knife around the edge, eventually peeling back the facing, which was lined with an opaque cloth of some type. I pulled out a folded piece of parchment, roughly 12 by 14 inches square and walked over to Marge's marble bar top and pulled up a stool.

Bella turned the lights on overhead and sat next to me. Various law enforcement types scurried and moved about us, but we ignored them. With great care, I unfolded the map, stopping briefly as the paper protested, escaping from its wrinkled state of aged repose. It was a hand-drawn map, with beautiful ink lettering and notations. I started by picking out landmarks, each with notations in cursive, offering further defining comments. It was sort of a diary: carefully kept and hidden, laying here unknown to generations of Carlyles. The secret lay literally within their grasp. The irony was astonishing. The rogue pastor never went looking in a bible, of all places. Perfect. I laughed out loud, the strain of the day easing out of me.

"I am guessing Henry produced this map and carefully hit it," I said. "I am sure he had traced a copy onto some sort of translucent paper, or copied the details onto something to take out on the trail." I felt a tremor go through me, now holding the tangible evidence for the detective work I had previously only postulated. Simon and the diary had added details and their own speculation, but herein lay before me proof. A historical document in its own right, truly amazing. More tiles clicked into place in my mind.

I stood. I had to go see Lauren. "I have to go."

"I know, Conn. Take all the time you need. But let's go find the rest of the treasure soon. I have to get out to my team and the others; we still have a busy night raiding labs, businesses, and houses."

I waved to Gene and Caleb, who were out mingling with their new compatriots. Time to roll again.

Chapter 42

My friends brought me back to Bella's, where I picked up my bag, the diary, and the few belongings I had, and let Grey hop in the back of the crew cab pickup with me. We stopped in L'Anse at my insurance agency and picked up a check for the replacement of my vehicle. It was a bit of a hassle, since my vehicle was in an impoundment lot somewhere, but Bella had pulled a few strings and gotten a few pictures taken, so my insurance company was able to declare it totaled. Understatement indeed.

We drove over to the used car lot, where I negotiated the purchase of another Ford F-150, a couple years old and decent for my use. As I walked out of the dealership with the keys and a temporary plate, I was greeted by Gene and Caleb sitting on the tailgate, drinking sodas and munching on chips.

"Do you guys ever stop eating?" I grinned at these two rascals, who had saved my life a few times now.

"Munch 'em while you got 'em, chief. Don't you remember that from training?"

"Um, no."

"You must have been nodding off during that session."

Gene mock-nudged Caleb. "What do you think we should

charge for saving his bacon yet again? How many times is this now? 12?"

Caleb was munching on the remnants of his bag of chips and looked at me thoughtfully. "13?"

"You are going to behave if we take off now?" Gene asked. "Methinks it wouldn't hurt to stick around and cover you for a few more days."

"You guys have done enough, and for the record, I think it is only four times."

Gene responded loftily, "You think? Some thanks we get."

"I will make sure you guys get some of the reward. As Moore goes down, there should be some settlement and whistleblower monies. You guys can have a little. I will get you a plaque, too."

"A little?" More raised eyebrows. "Don't worry Conn, your eternal gratitude and servitude is enough payment for us." Caleb could be droll. "If the plaque is solid gold, I will take it."

"I think you guys should get back to your families, give my best to Claire and Natalie. Kids, too." I handed over a small canvas bag with a few pounds of the silver coins they helped recover. "Make sure they get some of these souvenirs." I owed them that, and indeed much more.

We had our brief one-armed half-hugging and back slapping routine and said our goodbyes.

Gene waved through his open window and yelled out from the curb on US 41. "The seagull smasher is in the backseat of your new truck, with a few rocks should you need. See ya, bud."

Indeed, I did hate to see them go. I could feel some loose ends needing to be wrapped up.

But first, a road trip to see Lauren. I could always hope the threats to my well-being were over, but I doubted it. I opened the door to the truck, started the engine and looked back. The seagull smasher was in a case, but there was also a long, black canvas gear bag that had some heft to it. I unzipped a side pocket, pulled out a nice Smith and Wesson .357, and threw a few clips in the front seat next to me. Something was still in the air, and I hoped it wasn't more helicopters. I also wasn't entirely sure of the providence of all of the gear in the back, but I had learned with those gentlemen that it wasn't always best to make deep inquiries. Express gratitude, keep their phone numbers at hand, and stay armed and alert.

I pulled out on US 41 and headed southwest, into a setting sun and the coolness of a fall evening. Grey slept on the back seat, with his head hanging over the edge. I had the radio on softly, and weather reports indicated the season's first chance for measurable snow that evening, so I was glad I had four-wheel drive at my disposal. The dark grey truck was in decent shape and had new tires. I couldn't have been more anxious; the two-hour drive to Eagle River, Wisconsin seemed to take forever. I got out, stretched, let Grey do his thing, and then we hopped back into the truck.

I gave my name at the front desk and was gratified to have a uniformed guard escort me back to her room. Lauren lay in a hospital bed, an IV tube hooked up to her and a thin blanket pulled over her chest. She smiled wanly and dipped her head when I leaned forward to kiss her. I kissed her forehead and sat next to her in a metal chair.

"Why didn't you tell me you were still in Wisconsin?"

"From what I understand, you were running for your life. I had no way to contact you. I had neighbors out looking for you on four-wheelers. Nothing." She managed to get all of that out in one breath. Whew.

She had a point, not much I could have done with the knowledge anyway. It was a kick to the system that Moore and his gang found her and tried to use her against me.

"Conn, I told you that you were putting me at risk with this business and moved to avoid it. I was driving to Wisconsin to see my sister, when they . . . kidnapped me. Damn you, Conn. I told you to let this go."

"Move?" I asked. "We argued, and you left. You could have told me where you were. I can't believe you kept that from me. I was running for my life for the last week!" It seemed like months running, but hey.

"You had other issues, and I asked you to leave, and you wouldn't run. You are so stubborn!"

I brushed a lock of Lauren's hair from her face and touched her cheek. "I am sorry." A tear fell from her eye and dripped on the front of her hospital gown.

I reached over, held her hand, and she leaned back and wept. I remained silent and focused on her face.

Chapter 43

I stayed at the hospital with her for another day, and then we drove together to Grand Rapids in downstate Michigan. We went wide around Chicago to avoid the loop, and took our time, stopping to pick up sundries and food along the way. A few snowflakes were in the air as a front moved in, but the roads stayed dry. Lauren had rented a house a mile from her parents, and I nodded approval at the small rowhouse in a quiet cul-de-sac.

"You can sleep on the couch tonight, Conn."

I got it, I thought.

"Conn, I need some time. Can you give it to me? I am glad you are safe, and grateful you came to me. Go home, take care of your affairs, and then we can talk. Right now I still want the divorce, and these events haven't helped my thinking."

I had been there only a day and I was getting on Lauren's nerves. This hurt. But yes, I had things to wrap up. That evening, as the winds grew colder, I pulled out of the cul-de-sac and started heading north. By the time I reached the Mackinac Bridge into Upper Michigan, there were wind advisories, and to me it felt like they should close the bridge due to the 40-miles per hour gusts. I pulled off at the Holiday gas station in St. Ignace and dialed her phone. I got her answering machine.

"Bella, what are you up to tomorrow? Would you want to take a drive and maybe a hike? Call me."

And so she did. Tomorrow, I hoped, we would find more answers. A few things had been nagging at me. And we had the Bible-map. With my study, it looked like old Henry Laird had pin-pointed possible locations and died for it. He had been killed in the woods, having taken the precaution of hiding the map in his motel in Baraga. I was still surprised his brother John hadn't claimed it, but guessed that ancestors of the Moores had broken into the room and cleaned it out. The probate records indicated Henry had less than $200 in cash as his total net worth. He had sold his property the previous year for more than that. I could only surmise he was cleaned out, with some effects left as to arouse no suspicion surrounding the circumstances of his death. I could just see the good reverend walking out of the room with the Bible and piously telling the desk clerk or any officers that "Henry would've wanted the church to have his bible." I can only imagine the dismay at not finding anything of substance in the pages. But I guess this charlatan never really did find much of any substance in the pages of the book he pretended to espouse and represent.

Bella pulled into the driveway of the Lakeside Inn in Baraga the next morning. A heavy frost lay over the parking lot. I had my truck running. Grey wagged excitedly when he saw Bella.

She jumped in my truck passenger seat, unslinging a good size rucksack. She grinned and leaned across and gave my cheek a brush-kiss, more sisterly than romantic. I was okay with that for now.

"Remember the strange tombstone next to Carlyle's?" I asked. "With the inscription 'Rarely Hid In?' We were so caught up in the bible verses on his tombstone — it made only a passing impact on me."

"Yes. What about it?"

"Rarely Hid In. At first, I was thinking it related to the silver mine referenced on the tombstone. A clue that the silver was in plain sight. I was driving late last night when it hit me."

She looked across at me skeptically. She did that a lot. Didn't I earn any respect over the last week?

"Rarely Hid In," I repeated. "It is an anagram."

Bella gripped my arm as it hit her. "Holy Cow. Henry Laird."

"It would have been easier if they had used 'Hi Dry in Real." I laughed. "Then I would've known it was an anagram."

"So you were right. Henry is not buried adjacent to James Kyle. He is next to Carlyle. Wow."

She slugged my arm. Again.

"Could you stop doing that? Geez."

"Let's get this truck in gear. We have a cemetery to revisit." Grey barked happily in the back seat. He really liked our team. I think he thought she had treats for him, and there was a chance for a hike. He was probably right on both counts.

"We have one stop first before the cemetery," I said.

Damn. She was really good at the one-raised eyebrow thing.

Chapter 44

The Carlyle and anagram headstones were close to us as we entered the cemetery — down and to the right, on the oldest part. As we left the truck, I noticed a headstone that I had missed before. Henry Laird and James Kyle's headstones were still far up on the hill and on the left, but here was a half-broken similar headstone at the entrance to the old portion of the cemetery. Very interesting. I pointed it out to Bella, who smiled.

"Curiouser and curiouser," she said.

Very much so, we would return here.

We stopped at the anagram stone. I laughed when I circled the stone, looking for the name. I found it on the west side, away from our entry to the area. "Irving M. Waiting."

I paused. I.M. Waiting. I am waiting.

I hefted the short piece of half-inch rebar I had just purchased. I double gripped it like Excalibur, and thrust it into the ground in the center of the I.M. Waiting's place of repose. Nothing. I wrested it up and down, getting about six feet deep. I pulled it out and did my King Arthur routine again. A deep thrust, and then a few words inappropriate for a cemetery were uttered as my rebar thunked on something less than four feet down. Bella stood next to me, and she also took up the search.

We narrowed it down to a square yard footprint. Certainly not a coffin, and it was pretty shallow. It did feel like wood down there, but it did not have any give, like it was a box.

Bella commented. "We need to call the village and the Sheriff. I don't want to be a grave robber, or worse yet, be caught digging one up."

"This isn't a grave, Bella."

She wouldn't relent and threatened to use the rebar on me. I gave up.

While waiting for authorities and a reporter from the L'Anse Sentinel, we examined the old broken headstone at the entrance. It had a broken off top, just like Henry's. A small steel dowel had connected the lantern to the rest of the stone. We couldn't make much of it, so I went and got some paper from my duffel bag and used a small pencil I found in the glove compartment to make a rubbing. Interesting. No name, just another inscription. Was this cemetery filled with clues?

"Since we are waiting anyway, would you mind telling me how you met Gene and Caleb?"

I smiled at her. "That is a story that would take a long time to tell. Suffice it to say it is colorful. I owe my life to them, a few times over. I think they gave you a few details on our last mission before I retired."

"To have that kind of loyalty and friendship, I would assume you have acted in kind on occasion." She put a hand on my shoulder. "Tell me someday. Especially the part where they just happen to have a military-grade arsenal at hand. I am anxious to hear about that."

"No promises. Suffice it to say they are friends who helped take care of some bad things in a few bad places. Unsung, not even known to their families. But the right people know."

"Ex-military?"

"In a matter of speaking, yes."

"And you?"

"Township Historian."

"Before that? What about your time downstate?"

"Community College Librarian."

There, I got the eye rolling. It had been too long.

"C'mon, Conn, I liked them."

"They worked undercover, exposing human trafficking rings, and partook in a few other miscellaneous tasks. I can say no more."

"And you know them how?"

"Let's say we worked together on occasion. They saved my life more than once. "

"And it would be safe to say they owe you a few favors as well."

I grew serious. "We are beyond favors. It is about brotherhood, shared danger and respect."

A black pickup was pulling into the cemetery and rolled to a halt behind my vehicle. Two men got out and walked over to us.

"Steve, what are you doing here?" Bella looked surprised. "Checking up on us again?"

"What are you two doing back here? Find anything else, more clues?" Steve's stone face was inscrutable.

"I don't recall discussing clues with you, Steve," said Bella. "Seriously, what are you doing here? Who is he?"

She pointed to the thin man behind her old partner. He was all of six foot two, lean, black hair swept back from a widow's peak, and was wearing sunglasses and a short black cloth coat.

"I believe I can help with that," the unknown man said. "I retain a vital interest in the fruits of your arduous labors of the past week."

He had a nasally voice, not that I needed more reason to justify my instant dislike of him. My hand went to my belt for the pistol.

The man waved a hand, gesturing around him. "You really don't know who might be watching."

I was hating him more. Evidently another player had entered the mix. Scene Four, Act Two.

"I take it you are not a Moore or at least not a Moore anymore?"

"More or less incorrect." He didn't even crack a smile in responding. Dry sense of humor. "Let's just leave my involvement explained as a vital interest. But rest assured, it is in your best interest to share information with me. I have birthright and moral right to the treasure you are seeking."

Was that a Kentucky accent? I wasn't sure, the nasal quality to his voice was not only annoying, it masked any dialect. I could guess.

"Finerly or Strong?" I asked, thinking back to the names of the Confederates driving the wagons.

"Neither."

"Heinzman?" I persisted. He didn't respond. It had to be Heinzman, the trooper shot at the river.

Stone Face had a gun out and trained on us. "Tell him what we need to know about the treasure."

Bella looked shocked, I just stood there. I had figured out that he had to be the mole — he was too close to Bella — and someone had been feeding information to our hunters. As Bella's partner and confidant, he had an opportunity to keep up the charade.

"How many pieces of silver to sell us out, Steve?" She was angry. "Enough to throw away your career?"

He screwed up one side of his face — his evil side, I guess. I thought it was all or nothing, but part of him was trying to remain in control and keep up the pretense of being an officer. "Ten percent. Millions."

Bella didn't snort, but it was close. "But what if you die for the promise? What if they get rid of you?"

His façade was cracking a bit. I helpfully added, "I owe you a beating for the hospital attack." I smiled. "It wasn't you, but I know you either arranged or allowed it to happen. Two bad apples, Bella."

His response was concise and filled with invective. Suffice it to say, his feelings were clear.

The thin man interrupted. "Stop. We don't have much time. I have mobilized a mining and demolitions crew in Alston, and they are on standby now. Surely you know the location of the treasure. "

Bella was mentally killing Steve and stared at him with an intense hatred. "You tell him everything?"

He looked momentarily embarrassed. "He knew most of it anyway. The family has far-reaching ties."

"Do share. Lives are at stake here."

I responded with two unkind words, and Thin Man nodded at Stone Face, who put a shot at Bella's feet. We heard only a sharp hiss, and I saw it had a silencer.

"I will kill you for that, Steve." Her voice was flat, emotionless. She took a step forward.

I waved toward the tombstone. "Enough. The clue is on the stone. This isn't worth dying over."

Steve waved his gun, and Bella and I walked to the stone, where I knelt and traced the Bible verse references with a forefinger. "They both point to the mountain. See for yourself."

Thin Man came forward with his smart phone. A few taps. "They are right. Let's go for a ride. People are waiting. Someone sure was clever. No one put this together over the last 100 years."

I winked at Bella and stood, knees wet from the morning dew. I hoped they didn't see the rebar or the small holes in the adjacent plot belonging to I.M Wating, our new close friend. Apparently, they had been following a tracker on Bella and had just arrived.

I pointed at the black truck. "Let's go. I want resolution. And credit for finding the treasure."

We were both in the backseat, behind a wire-mesh partition. Seems like Steve had the keys to an un-marked vehicle. We took the first few minutes in silence, and Thin Man turned in the front seat.

"I assume you know where it is now?" They had taken our handguns and phones. I took Bella's hand and gave her my best confident look. She squeezed back.

"I have a good idea. The clues on the stone and the book both point to the mountain."

"Let us proceed and bring closure." Thin Man leaned his head back against the headrest and closed his eyes. He was presenting well with the whole confidence game.

Chapter 45

Thin Man had indeed assembled a large fleet of equipment and a cadre of miners. The backwoods around the base of the mountain was wet, and steam rose from rumbling excavators and various drill rigs. No sense arguing — this stuff would be needed some day.

"We had searched here along the southeast face, thinking the wagon came from the south on the old logging and Indian roads," he said. "But looking at some old maps of the area, he had to have come down from South Laird Road and the area called Silver." He nodded impatiently. "And …"

"I think the cave was on the north side," I responded. "Maybe not even a cave. Could have been ravine or washout."

"You seem to be singularly well informed, Mr. Constantine."

A small group of hard-bitten men surrounded me, wearing a mixture of reflective fluorescent gear and winter jackets. They each had a beard and seemed to be cousins or just had worked together too long. Equipment was idling around me, and I led off with a quick pace. I grabbed a map from one of the operators and stabbed a finger ahead to the north. All for the show now. "Walk with me, Judas."

Steve ignored me, but did move up to keep pace, while still far enough away to keep me from jumping him. With the look Bella was giving his back, I was surprised he hadn't dropped dead.

We came to a cleft in the face, a narrow defile leading out from a small plateau about 50 feet high. I gestured at a sloping face of a jagged rockfall. The escarpment was no more than 20 feet high where it trailed off to us at the ground. I gestured north into the level forest floor stretching out to the north. I held out the map, and Thin Man peered at it.

"I would start here, moving into the face," I directed. "The explosion he set to hide the wagon would have left a rockfall similar to this." Steve and Thin Man looked skeptical. "Surely, someone would have dug here previously." I glanced at Bella, who clearly could not believe I was cooperating with these clowns. "The diary said he set multiple charges around the base." I was good at lying through my teeth. "The thieves may have given up and followed the trail up to Limestone Mountain. The blasting would have been easier there."

The group of operators shrugged as one, and a squat, bearded man spoke up. "What are your orders, Mr. Heinzman?"

Ah, there it was. Now the pieces came together. Impatiently, Thin Man waved a hand and pointed at the rock-fall. "Dig."

The forest echoed with the sounds of rumbling equipment as pieces staggered into motion. One excavator had a bucket-arm that was clearing trees ahead of the other pieces moving

252

into position. Two others started clawing at the base; one had a hydraulic hammer that went to work. A drill rig pulled next to us, a monolith in the small wilderness glen, waiting to strike at the face as well — a hornet waiting to sting.

The assemblage hammered and banged away for most of the afternoon. Thin Man — Mr. Heinzman — stood next to me. "It should be close if it is here," I said. "He couldn't have been carrying much for charges with him. He didn't have time to arrange more. I want to be closer; this is my find to make."

"Like hell it is. You have only been a participant for a few weeks. We have hunted for a century. This is for me and my family. Cover them." This he spat out to a miner behind us, who produced a pistol from the pocket of his jacket. It was interesting to me that we had two sets of enemies, each with seemingly large resources at their command. Well, we had taken down one. One to go, with the rest of the treasure at stake. And our lives.

Heinzman scrambled up the slope with Steve close behind. They were obviously intent on being at the scene. I yelled, "There can't be much left of the wagon under all that rock."

Stone Face flipped me off from his perch up on the hill. They were both pointing at something, and an arm was waved to move the drill-rig into position. The beast blew black smoke and engaged the tracks, walking up the shelved path created by the excavators. Hydraulic controls kicked into play, and the long needle stood poised to strike at the heart of the slope. Apparently, they intended to drill in preparation for placing charges to blow the rock pile at the base of the mountain. The high-pitched whine made us set our teeth. We watched in silence for nearly an hour when the drill withdrew and adjusted, ready for another strike. Apparently, they were going to drop charges down. I reached over and took Bella's arm, pulling her away from the mass of rock before us. I put a finger to my lips, out of sight of our guard. We began to edge away, moving slowly backward. Our guard had become transfixed by the drilling and was focusing on the silhouettes of the massed equipment.

The explosion of rock ripped apart the trees around us, and a geyser of grey and black spouted into the air above us. We were thrown to the ground by a thunderclap of sound. Our guard had fallen, stunned by the blast, and I took the opportunity to pick up the fallen weapon and put a round into him. I pretty much made sure he stayed down.

The drill rig was balanced awkwardly, pitched back against the slope. The operator was either unconscious or dead, as the front of the enclosed cab had been blown away. There was no sign of our captors.

Bella was stumbling towards the slope when I grabbed her. We saw a hand reach up from the top of the pile of rock, and then a bloody face materialized, barely recognizable in the haze. The drill rig swayed wildly, the drilling arm swung to its side, downhill in our direction, groaning in an unearthly manner, screeching like a wounded vulture. The figure was trying to crawl away towards us, away from the crater. The screeching intensified as the giant toppled and fell into a cloud of dust.

We found Heinzman shortly thereafter, impaled by the huge bit that had broken off in the explosion. His face was a mix of fear and shock.

Bella was at my shoulder. "Screw Him."

My goodness, my protégé was growing up. Sarcasm, bad puns . . . I was a great influence and teacher. At least I didn't have to listen to Heinzman's voice anymore. Or listen to his threats. Good riddance.

We saw Steve's body a good distance away from the blast.

"What in the hell was that?" Bella was staring at the crater as the surviving miners peeled away rock, trying to unearth the remnants of the two excavators. Both operators had been killed. We stepped away, and I kept the pistol trained on the men, but they were too busy to care about us. They were still at their labor when law enforcement showed up. Bella had found a radio in one of the maintenance trucks and called in the cavalry.

The crew surrendered without incident, but requested they finish the excavation. The bowels of the Earth trembled again, with another explosion, smaller this time, which echoed in the air. They gave up then.

Bella and I stood, covered in sweat and dust, watching the cleanup operation. Michigan State Police officers came and paid us their respects, and asked us to come in later for a report.

I wanted to stay. I had my theory on the explosives, and it related directly to the Confederate spy effort this mission was intended to support. But it could wait for another day.

"Conn, you are crazy, there could be another explosion," said Bella "Let's leave this to the experts."

"They were the experts," I said. "Look at what happened to them."

I walked over to the crater on the edge of the plateau and slowly made my way down the jumble of rock. I swept a few stones with my hand, brushing away the grey dust. Bella yelled down at me and I ignored her, and suddenly she slid down the loose shale, grinding to a halt a few yards away from me.

I bent over and picked up a small misshapen rectangular piece of rock, held it out before me, and looked over at Bella.

"Good for you, wise guy, you found a rock." Clearly, in her mind, I had lost my mind. I smiled, then breathed out a puff of air, and then another.

The face of the rock glowed with a yellow light, and an amber arc caught the ray of sunlight peering through the overcast sky above.

Bella was speechless. There was a first time for everything.

Epilogue

Two years have passed since we made the remarkable find of the treasure — the Lost Wagon that changed my life. It astonished many that they had lived almost within sight of it for decades. I declined most interviews and requests to discuss the findings, but did put my hand to recording the events that led to the finding. We found, or rather the archeologists we brought in from Michigan Tech found, over 100 bars of gold. Explosives experts were also brought in from the Tilden Mine in Negaunee. They worked with brushes and metal detectors, exposing bricks malformed by the explosion. They also found shards of cast iron and wood, which were taken to the Michigan State Police crime lab for testing.

The wagon had been made with white oak, and lab results showed it was from Kentucky. The metal shards were examined by some explosives experts and thought to be, as I hypothesized, Courtenay torpedoes. The drill bit had sparked on a stone and ignited the small explosive charges.

Moore Industries went into bankruptcy, with pieces of the empire sold off to creditors. Thaddeus was tried for conspiracy and murder. I did not attend the court hearings but did testify at sentencing. He was given 40 years, and lasted just over one year in prison, where he died of a heart attack.

The bodies of Eunice and Yancy were found in a ravine behind their property. I had Eunice buried next to her brother, my Uncle Jack. I kept up the plots, and did place one flower on her grave, understanding she had been caught up in a whirlwind of desperation and acted poorly.

Law enforcement, including state police and both Houghton and Baraga County sheriff's departments, spent nearly a year cleaning up the drug operations in Upper Michigan and Northern Wisconsin. Four former executives at Moore Logistics were indicted, including Thad's oldest son, Weston. The operation had included money laundering, extortion, and evidence of human trafficking. A dozen individuals in Laird Township alone were arrested, and plea deals struck. A confession was made by Frankie to the killings of Davey, his brother Josh, and Zack; he was given 60 years and avoided the death penalty. The Haakanen brothers pleaded guilty to attempted murder along with drug possession and transport, and are currently both in Jackson State Prison serving 20-year sentences.

Marge was tried and given 20 years. She committed suicide by hanging six months into her sentence. Her home was sold by the State under seizure laws and proceeds went to two local women's shelters.

I took the reward money and used it to build a new public library in Alston, named after my Uncle Jack. I purchased property near the old 'downtown' area at the old Mineral Range Depot location. It was a fine structure, masonry bearing, with a gleaming white, prefinished siding exterior. A tribute to Jack and his thoughts about reflecting the nature of the interior on the outside. I also would not have to look forward to painting it every year. His books became the centerpiece of the collection, and I was gratified to have a number of volumes on local history donated for the use of township residents as well. It pained me a bit, but I used many of Marge's collection in the library as well. I felt it was better to have some good come from the evil she had wrought in her life.

I rebuilt my home on a new foundation closer to the West Branch of the Sturgeon. I installed an elaborate sprinkler system, fire alarms, and security system. I also installed a siege tower and installed gun ports on the exterior. Okay, I am kidding about the last two components. I also re-sided the old sauna, which had survived both fires on the site. I still took the opportunity to enjoy a couple saunas per week. In memory of Jack, I would, on occasion, elicit too much steam from the rocks and chase myself outside. Grey would lie patiently in the cool-off room, and bark joyfully whenever I raced out, and would into the creek with me during the summer months. We both missed Satch, and I would find Grey often sniffing around the property: I think he too found places to reminisce about his old friend. The sauna steam also afforded me reflection time, and found myself adrift for hours, healing and sweating away memories, aches, and the pain of loss. I thought often of my parents and wondered about what they would have thought of me as I grew into adulthood. I hope they would have been proud of me. However, since I wasn't sure how proud I was of myself, my mental jury was out on the subject. I let it be.

I still kept Simon's coin with me — the very piece of silver that had started me on this life-altering path. The balance of the silver had been donated to the Museum of the Confederacy, with equal parts going to the Smithsonian and the Houghton County Historical Museum. I didn't want, nor felt right, about keeping any of it. Bella kept a few coins, as did Gene and Caleb. They managed to show up every few months and enjoy a few glasses of bourbon and some beautiful sunsets in Laird Township. They also faithfully promised to keep their stories for my future children all G-rated and paint me in the best-possible heroic light in all of their tales. Like that was going to happen . . . the stories, I mean. Children hopefully someday.

I had a stack of speaking engagements to consider: emails, calls, and letters arrived weekly for chances to speak at historical societies, conferences, and to appear on book tours. I did want to help the State of Indiana Tourism Board refurbish the signage and interpretation along the John Hunt Morgan Heritage Trail, and now we had a chance to put markers up in Wisconsin, and now Michigan.

Lauren and I continued to work on picking up the broken pieces of what our relationship was and would manifest itself to be. She moved into a home in L'Anse and resumed working at Michigan Tech. We talked on the phone every few nights. The divorce papers never came, but the specter hung over us.

I was stunned one day on an exploratory trip to find the remains of a massive old White Pine on the edge of our property; lightning had long ago struck and killed the tree, splitting it down the center. It must have been at least four foot in diameter, and judging by the rotted remains of the branches and trunk, it had been a massive tree. About twelve feet still remained, and I found a railroad spike eight feet off the ground, stained by the years and nearly rusted away. I almost fell into a hole in the ground 40 feet away, working my way through poplar trees; I could make out the roughly square outline of a cellar. It chilled me to my core, and I could feel the evil rising out of the ground around me. Astonishing how time and coincidence wrap around each other. They must have taken the man down, removed the spike and left it for a reminder. And a warning.

I thought again about Ezekiel, my next project was to find out about what happened to him. Sara Corbett, I found in my research, married a mining man, and lived for many years on College Avenue in Houghton. I ran a search on her family and found one son, Ezekiel Wilson. She did not forget. I found one Wilson living in Houghton and resolved to visit them one day and tell them a story. In Ezekiel's memory, I sent wire transfers to a number of women's shelters, trusted counselors, crisis workers, and a few agencies. I only attached one word to the donations: Zeke.

Brenda had gotten back to me from the museum and indicated she had not found a Susan at the Catholic Mission, but had done more checking and found a Native woman named Suzanne Levesque that worked at the Methodist mission in L'Anse. Her phone message also indicated she was looking forward to having coffee someday to catch up. I had smiled; I owed her that at least.

Grey and I still took many walks in both the Silver Mountain and Limestone Mountain areas and traversed the many miles of the old Mineral Range Railroad grade. We often were joined by Bella, who had gotten a pit bull mix from the Copper Country Humane Society. Grey was wary at first of the puppy, but now they enjoyed romping together, rolling and wrestling in the leaves and grass along our many paths. Bella and I still were just friends. She intimated once that she and Judas, I mean Steve, had gone out a few times, although she was still recovering from his betrayal. Time would tell. I enjoyed her company and she enjoyed my wonderful sense of humor. Well, that last part may be an exaggeration. She kept coming back, so maybe it was an acquired taste.

I did surprise her one evening. I promised her a home-cooked dinner, and promised it would be platonic, and she came over in a beautiful yellow sundress, with her hair brushed back. She had applied makeup very faintly, and I smelled a rose-like perfume when I hugged her at the door. The roast beef was still cooking, and I invited her to sit down on the couch. I had lit candles, and Grey came and lay quietly at our feet. On the coffee table, I had a small folder, which I handed to her. It had an old-fashioned string-tie clasp, which she slowly unwound while giving me her inimitable sidelong glance. Her half-smile was tinged with curiosity, I prayed the contents would indeed prove worthy of the presentation and anticipation.

She gasped upon reading the first lines of the opening page. Genealogy Report for Isabella Suzanne Anderson. I had her full attention. She was scanning the lines I had typed from my research of the past month. She scanned the list of her parents, grandparents, and great-grandparents, nodding thoughtfully. Her lips parted a bit, and she breathed in slowly as she flipped the page.

Great-grandparents: Suzanne Anderson, née Levesque, birthplace: Sault Sainte Marie, Michigan; and Thomas "Mc-Ghee" Anderson, birthplace: Lexington, Kentucky.

Her eyes widened, and I watched her face for a reaction. Grey even was still for a moment, gazing up at her expectantly. She put a hand to her mouth and looked over at me, the question on her glowing face. It was my turn to nod. He had made it. He never went home. He let the treasure lie; knowing the resurrection of it could cause questions that he could not answer, and love compelled him to keep the secret.

A tear ran down her cheek, and she reached up and wiped it away, slowly shaking her head from side to side. I reached over and turned to the last page of the report.

Cause and location of death: Natural causes. 1889 and 1893. Silver Location, Michigan.

After she left for the evening, I sat on the porch of my new home, watching the distant embers of stars start to glow in the fading twilight. I had a glass of bourbon sitting waiting at my left hand, while my right stroked Grey who lay beside me. The violence that had encompassed my life seemed a distant memory, but I still vividly recalled the licking fires and their hunger to destroy. I also knew that these fires had refined me, honing the steel awareness of life and the precious gifts of awareness and immediacy. I also reflected on the rebirth that followed the destruction, and the possibility someday of being a father to a child that could be raised here, who, like me, could feel wonder and amazement at the quiet miracle of night and the opportunity to take its cloak upon oneself, to cleanse and heal. To know memory is a precious thing, and secrets, though often dangerous, have much to reveal to those who took the time to listen.

***

On the far edge of the field, I watched as the fading flame of daylight caught the top of a giant White Pine, painting the uppermost branches with a golden light. I could see, even at this distance, that the branches were stretched out, almost at an impossible length, and it seemed as if they were arms lifted in prayer and supplication. The sun blessed the beseeching limbs with a benediction, touching them with the tender rays of mercy and promise, and then fell silently beyond the western horizon in a breathless whisper.

Author's Note

This book is a work of fiction, but many of the main story elements are based in truth, or at least documented mysteries. The town of Alston is indeed real, as are many of the creeks, rivers, roads, and physical features depicted in the story. Creative license with some geographic features were taken to help drive the plot.

The source of the naming of Silver Mountain, the Silver River, and the settlement of Silver are indeed shrouded in some mystery. The designation appears on maps as early as 1860, long before major settlement of Laird Township took place. Most of the initial homesteading took place in the latter part of the 19th century. The legend of the Native American spirit that guards Silver Mountain is true, although the elements relating to this legend were fabricated for the narrative.

Henry Laird, a central part of the narrative, was indeed a mystery. The details of his Civil War service are presented factually, as are the mysteries of his death, tombstone, and property dealings. He was a driving force in creating what would come to be Laird Township and served as its first supervisor for three terms. He is an enigmatic character and I continue to research the life of this locally-influential person.

The town of Alston and some of the characters appearing in the early 1900s' portion of the story are indeed real. Joseph Alston and his brother David did capitalize on the promise offered by the running of the new South Branch of the Mineral Range Railroad through the town of Laird, which they bought up and renamed after themselves. David never lived in his namesake town, and Joseph would meet a tragic end, dying in an insane asylum in Newberry, Michigan, where had lived the last many years of his life with his wife Eva.

The lean-to where poor Sara Corbett was held is based on ruins of a foundation found on my property, where there is old root cellar and remnants of a homestead of unknown origin. The Mineral Range Railroad bed running through the west end of the same property has a siding named Corbett on old records, with the given name having no known source, and thus giving rise to the story device.

Forced prostitution has been documented in many frontier towns, with kidnappings a very real occurrence. Nearby Ontonagon County was said to have many brothels in which women were held against their will: mining, logging, and mills fueled the trade, with thousands of men exercising their dark desires.

General John Hunt Morgan was indeed a cavalry leader during the American Civil War in the service of the Confederate Army, and he was known for his raids into Kentucky and Tennessee. His "Great Raid" through Kentucky, Indiana, and Ohio took place in June and July of 1863. He violated the orders of his commanding officers, specifically General Braxton Bragg, by crossing the Ohio River into the North. Various reasonings have been offered for his Raid, including a boost to Southern morale that was at low ebb in July of 1863 (defeats at Gettysburg on July 3rd and the fall of the Mississippi fortress city of Vicksburg occurred during this raid), as well as a desire to "bring the war to the north" and draw Union forces from pursuit of Bragg's Confederates' withdrawal from north central Tennessee to Chattanooga. Morgan was a fine horseman and representative of the Southern ideal knight or gentleman cavalier, greatly admired by many, especially women. He would surrender to superior Union forces at the end of his Great Raid in Northeastern Ohio after leading thousands of Northern troopers on a chase that lasted [[45 days]]. His Great Raid covered over 1,000 miles and diverted the attentions of over 110,000 men throughout the territory. Rumors of treasure buried along the route have swirled around for 150 years, including loot seized on the raid and buried by Ohioans fearful of having their valuables stolen. I strongly recommend driving all or part of the Heritage Trail which follows the entire route he and his men travelled — it is a must for Civil War and history buffs. I have driven it and the route underscores just how incredible the Raid itself was.

John Hunt Morgan would be killed on his last Raid in Greenville, Tennessee, shot in the back by a Union trooper named Andrew Campbell when Union troops surrounded a home in which he was staying in 1864.

There was a large amount of activity on the part of the Confederate Secret Service throughout the war, with a number of operatives based in Canada. Crossings from Windsor, Ontario to Detroit, Michigan were commonplace. Southern spies also were interested in and postulated attacks on the Soo Locks and stopping the shipment of copper, which was vital to the Union war effort in the production of brass used in buttons, shell casings, cannon, and other machines of war. Records show that at some points during the Civil War, over 85% of the copper used in the north came from Michigan's Copper Country.

Alston and Laird Township have both also had a colorful history: robbery, murder, gambling dens, speakeasies, and vices of many kinds have been documented. I believe the ghosts of many untold fortunes still walk in the forests and fields of this area and one can hear the echoes of stories and lost treasure if one takes the time to listen.

***

As a final note to truth being stranger than fiction: near the completion of this novel, I found some old hand-drawn maps and an enlarged aerial photo from 1960 of what appears to be the Sturgeon Gorge Area among some papers left to me by my father, Ronald Seppanen. He had also detailed some locations of property in sketches and on some United States Geographic Survey maps from 1955. I remember his intense interest in local history and lost homesteads. He loved to walk in the woods and drive two-track roads. It is my hope that he would enjoy this fictional narrative if he were alive today. My interest in history, reading, and love for maps and Upper Michigan comes from him.

Thank you for reading, all my best.

Tim Seppanen

Acknowledgements

A writer writes in solitude but is inspired, advised, guided, and amused by friends and family. My thanks to the following:

First and foremost thanks to my daughter, Aurora, and my wife, Michelle, also an early draft reader.

My mother, Marlene Hilman and Raymond Hilman.

My sister, Rachel, and Gerry Bode.

Derek Juntunen, a great writer, reader, and above all, the friend who taught me so much about the art of living, endurance, and hope amidst suffering. This book is for him and for his unfinished and unpublished works from his short but immensely influential and inspirational life. The emotional ripples of the figurative reach from his wheelchair, spread out and echo quietly and impactfully even today, 20 years later.

Duane Rantala for a lifetime of friendship; we grew up reading, collecting, and exchanging books. This book is for also for him for having seen my first work, "The Quintessential Allocation," in high school. Finally, Duane. Thank you for all the years.

Delos Wilbur was a first draft reader of this book, I am grateful for his input and cleaning up "cinema sins." He is and has been a close friend for three and a half decades, as well as a travel and history tramping partner to a few dozen countries.

Jerry Juntunen, who I was fortunate enough to work with in construction, and who also is a history tramping, bluff climbing and dedicated reader and research partner…along with being a close friend.

John Haeussler is a published author and close friend who was also an early draft reader. Thank you for all the friendship along with history and writing discussions.

Brandon Carter: Battlefield tramper, scholar, lawyer, history resource, father to Thomas, and friend.

Dave Roth.

Don and Chris Weiss.

Cliff Nichols.

Ron Stevens.

Louis L'Amour.

Alistair MacLean.

Nelson DeMille.

Jack Higgins.

Greg Iles.

Lastly, my thanks to the proofreader of this book. She came aboard after the first draft was completed, and I am very appreciative of her effort, insight, and kind direction.